Stepping to the table, he pulled out the chair next to hers and she jumped, nearly dropping her book.

He grinned at her. Somehow his catching her off-guard made her seem more... real.

"You scared me half to death," she said.

"I apologize," he said, though his elation at seeing her overshadowed any regret at startling her. "May I?" he asked, indicating the chair.

"Of course," she said, seeming to shake off her surprise. "Can I get you something to drink?"

He almost said yes. He wanted anything she offered. But caught himself. "I can't drink tonight."

She looked askance at him. "But you're in a tavern."

"I know," he said, "What can I say?"

"It's because you had too much last night," she said.

He nodded slowly. That was a good enough explanation. For the time-being. Right now he wanted to know about her.

"What's your name?" she asked.

He raised an eyebrow. And perhaps she wanted to know about him.

"I need to add you to the list of members," she added quickly.

"Bradley Becquerel," he told her. "But I haven't paid my membership. Do you take credit?"

That elicited an odd expression on her face. "I took care of it."

"I can pay," he put a hand in his pocket to pull out his money clip.

She touched his other arm lightly on his sleeve. "We don't take credit anyway, so truly, don't worry about it."

WHEN THE STARS ALIGN

WHEN THE STARS ALIGN

THE BECQUERELS

KATHRYN KALEIGH

To learn more about Kathryn Kaleigh, visit

www.kathrynkaleigh.com

Kathryn Kaleigh

CHAPTER 1

*B*radley Becquerel hated Mardi Gras.

But here he was, crushed among the throngs of people, most of them staggering with intoxication as the darkness of an early evening storm settled over the city of New Orleans.

His new client, Ian McGregor had insisted he stay for the three-day weekend. Male bonding, he'd said. There wasn't much male bonding going on when Ian and the other two associates had gotten lost in the crowd over an hour ago.

Bradley had spent the first thirty minutes of that hour looking for them, then decided to make his way back to the hotel. Unfortunately, he could barely walk without literally stepping on someone's toes and being elbowed with every step. Besides, the Pat O Hurricane he'd had earlier had left him needing a drink of water.

With the noise of people and discordant jazz music, he couldn't even hear his own thoughts.

Lightening flashed above the crowd causing the din to increase with screams of surprise, but it was the thunder that thinned the crowd. The thunder that sounded more like an explosion than a mere storm.

After weaving his way through the moving crowd to the sidewalk, he passed the doors of the Place d'Armes hotel, and, after dodging a particularly loud trio of singing drunk college students undaunted by the sudden flood of raindrops, ducked through the next large wooden door. The establishment's name, Le Bon Temps Roule, was engraved at eye level on a bronze plaque on the heavy oak door.

Stepping inside, he was immediately struck by the quietness of the bar. It must have state of the art insulation to block out the cacophony of noise from the street. Other than the faint notes of a piano drifting from a back room, there wasn't even any loud music inside. There were only men sitting around in groups at small tables. Cigar smoke created a haze that prevented him from seeing only a few feet in front of him. He wiped his eyes with his sleeve, but the quietness provided enough relief that he could handle the discomfort of the smoke.

Perhaps he'd stumbled into a private party. Or a smoker's club. Like most places in the country, New Orleans had only a few public places left to enjoy a cigar and most of those were outside. Had he wandered into a private home?

Only a few glanced up as he passed. Some of the men were intent on their private conversations, others engrossed in the cards they held in their hands.

Bradley spotted the outline of the bar toward the left and navigated his way there. Only two other men sat on the row of barstools, huddled together in conversation to his left. He sat at the first stool he came to, near the center of the bar and, squinting through the smoke, examined his surroundings.

The men were all dressed in formal attire. A one hundred eighty degree change from the t-shirts and jeans on the street. Though he was wearing his uniform of black slacks and white oxford shirt, he was sorely underdressed.

A young male server, dressed all in white, carried a tray to one of the tables.

"How can I help you, Sir?"

Brad jerked his attention back to the bar. And his pulse quickened with surprise and immediate…intrigue. Her accent was soft and… French.

He stared into the greenest eyes he had ever seen. Her lips were plush, curved into a pleasant smile – her teeth perfectly straight and white. Her skin, smooth and pale, was framed by long ebony hair swirling around her shoulders.

It was all he could see of her features. She wore a Mardi Gras mask, covering just her eyes and the top of her nose. It appeared to be crafted from delicate white lace, tied around her head with a ribbon.

She lifted one elegant eyebrow and tilted her head to the side. "Perhaps you've had too much," she observed.

"Yes," Bradley managed to croak. "Water."

She poured water into a glass, a secret knowing smile on her lips.

Bradley wanted to see the rest of her face. Her voice and her eyes beckoned to him like a siren's song, but would she be as beautiful without the mask?

His gaze glued to hers, he gulped the water.

She watched him quizzically, that secret amusement playing about her lips.

"You're not from here," she whispered.

"No," he said, keeping his voice low to match hers. "Is this a private club?"

Her gaze skittered around the room. Back to his. "Yes," she said with a shrug.

"But I can be here?"

"We welcome everyone," she said, her smile confused.

"You just…" He swallowed a bubble of laughter. Perhaps he had had too much.

"Miss Lafleur?" A man to his left called out.

She held his gaze another moment, then turned and, retreating into the haze, walked several feet to stand in front of the man who had summoned her.

Lafleur. An old name. Old money.

While she opened a bottle and poured their drinks, he noticed that she wore a floor-length dress in a deep green, matching her eyes. As she worked, he studied the room's reflection in the mirror lining the wall in front of him.

The haziness created by the cigar smoke created an other-worldly atmosphere. For merely a moment, he experienced a flash of vertigo. It was gone so quickly, he decided he must have imagined it.

CAMILLE LAFLEUR HAD HER FATHER WRAPPED AROUND HER little finger. It was the only explanation for him letting her work in the tavern during Mardi Gras.

As long as you keep your mask on.

Nonetheless, the men knew who she was. This was well illustrated by the fact that they didn't hesitate to call her by name.

She wouldn't tell her father.

Since this was Friday, she had four more days to work. He'd agreed only to let her work through Mardi Gras, then the masks would come off and she would go back to being a proper young lady. Under normal circumstances, a lady never went into the tavern after dark.

She sighed. At least here she had something interesting to do. She kept the books during the day. It was natural to want to see actual business taking place.

Besides, she hated the mundane balls. Always the same handful of men vying for her hand.

Men she adamantly turned away. Despite her father's

insistence that at age eighteen, she needed to take a husband and have a child to carry on the bloodline. In the four years that had passed, he had all but given up on getting her wed.

Though she had two brothers, it was unlikely either of them would be married soon. Both of them had saddled up and went to Texas to fight Comanches. If she could have found a way, she would have gone with them.

Instead, she was forced to stay behind. Needing something to occupy her time, her father allowed her to take over the bookkeeping. The tavern during the winter months and the plantation during the summers.

All three of her father's children, it seemed, had a rebellious spirit.

According to her father they took after their mother.

As she uncorked the French wine, she watched the stranger from the corner of her eye. He wore odd clothes. No jacket. His shirt was white, but he had a narrow silver cravat tied tightly round his neck. It looked, to her, a bit uncomfortable.

And he wore no mask.

The whole point of Mardi Gras was to wear a mask to conceal one's identity.

It only worked, she thought sardonically, if the people didn't know who you were to start with.

Take this man sitting in front of her. He had absolutely no idea who she was – mask or no no mask.

And… even though he didn't wear a mask, she didn't know him.

She sighed.

If wearing a mask was what it took to give her permission to do something exciting and keep away from the interminable balls, wear the mask she would.

She went back to stand in front of the stranger. "You look hungry," she said.

"Do I?"

"Yes." She turned and pulled on a cord. Marcus appeared from the back in less than two minutes. "Bring this man something to eat."

"Yes ma'am," the boy said and rushed through a door behind the bar.

"Where are you from?" she asked, staring into his blue eyes. He looked different from the other men – and not just his clothing. His dark brown hair was short. He was clean-shaven. His teeth were white...and perfectly straight.

"Monroe," he said.

She'd not heard of Monroe, but no matter. Many people visited New Orleans from small settlements. What was it that was so different about him? She couldn't quite sort it out. He looked... out of place.

Marcus returned with a plate of catfish smothered in piquant sauce - one of her favorites, and set it in front of him.

She poured a glass of red wine into a glass and slid it next to his plate. His eyes widened with the first bite. "Spicy," he said, picking up the glass.

"Do you like it?"

"It's wonderful. I've never had anything like it."

She smiled and he froze, his fork in mid-air.

Perhaps it was the mask. She reached up to remove it, but remembered her father's words. *As long as you keep the mask on, you can work downstairs in the tavern behind the bar.*

She had quickly agreed.

I'm serious Camille. If the mask comes off, I'll pull you out of the tavern.

She lowered her hand. Kept the mask on.

She hadn't bothered reminding her father that she was the best barkeep he had. And... he didn't even have to pay her. She and her brothers had spent countless hours during the day playing barkeep. Then, when she was old enough, she had memorized all the drinks.

Her father was a pushover for her, but only as far as her safety went.

Besides she was having more fun than she'd had since her brothers left.

Marcus barely had time to get upstairs and back down before he reappeared at her elbow. "Mistress Camille, your father said it's time for you to come upstairs."

CAMILLE LAFLEUR. A MOST FITTING NAME IF EVER THERE HAD been one. With no more than a backward glance over her shoulder, she disappeared out of his life.

An older, bearded man in formal attire appeared to be her replacement. "Can I get you anything, Sir?" he asked.

He shook his head. "Is... Miss Lafleur's shift over?"

The new barkeeper scowled at him. "Miss Lafleur will not be back tonight. My name is David. Is there something I can get for you?"

"No," Bradley said, reaching into his front pocket for his money clip. "I'd like to pay my tab."

"It's included in your membership," the man said, picking up a towel to wipe the top of the bar.

"My membership." Bradley decided to let that go for the moment. He would come back in the morning and straighten all this out. Perhaps purchase a membership. Right now, he needed to get back to his hotel in case Ian was looking for him. Disappearing into the crowded streets of New Orleans probably wasn't creating such a good impression. Mixing New Orleans and work was never a good idea. Especially during Mardi Gras season.

He crossed the smoky room, opened the door, and stepped back into the noise and the crowds. He'd been gone, what, maybe an hour, but it was like he hadn't been gone at all.

As he stepped into the street, toward, hopefully, his hotel, his phone began to ping.

He pulled his iPhone out of his pocket and stared at it. He had nine missed calls, four phone messages, and several text messages.

Even though it was obviously turned on, he checked the volume. He must not have had any phone service inside the building. Shrugging it off, he listened to the four messages from his new client. They were across town – at a bar. Sidestepping a group of tourists, he dashed back a quick message. *Went back to hotel. See you in the morning.* Now all he had to do was find the hotel.

Bradley knew not to ask too many questions of his clients. He also knew that a good pilot had a short memory. A short memory meant more repeat business.

He was scheduled to fly them back to Houston on Sunday morning. That most likely meant he had tomorrow to himself. Although New Orleans wasn't his favorite place, he now had a purpose. He planned to find out exactly who this Camille Lafleur was and find out how to become a member of her private club.

Bradley found his way back to the hotel after following his phone's GPS for awhile, then stopping to ask for directions. He was much better at finding his way around in the air than in a crowded city.

Bradley went upstairs to his room, plugged in his phone, changed into his shorts and T-shirt, and landed on the bed before falling asleep.

The next morning, he woke sprawled across the bed, bed linens mostly in the floor. Though he didn't remember details, he knew he'd had nightmares again. The bad dreams had started just over a year ago with what he had come to think of as the disappearance of his sister.

They had been close. However, when he had begun the

grueling hours required to earn his pilot's license, they hadn't been as involved in each others lives.

Then she had disappeared.

Stepping into the shower, the hot water blasting on his head, he allowed his thoughts to settle.

And they settled on Camille Lafleur.

Today he would use GPS to get back to the bar. What was the name of it? Le Bon Temps Roule. Right next door to the Place d'Armes hotel.

He wanted to see Camille without her mask. He wanted to talk to her again. Bradley had dated his share of girls before. But this instant attraction was a new experience. He'd thought love at first sight was a myth. He thought love was something that grew over the years. Like his grandparents had.

The death of his grandmother, Vaughn, had hit the family hard. Especially his grandfather.

Bradley reluctantly turned off the hot shower. It was time to get his day started. He wanted to navigate the city before the tourists woke up.

He threw on some jeans and a sweatshirt. He didn't anticipate seeing his clients today. They would probably sleep until noon. Then start drinking again.

Bradley had never suffered from the allure of intoxication. Thank God he'd overcome genetics. His intoxication came from the feeling of flying high above the world. No one there but him. Of course, solo flights didn't pay for themselves, so those were few and far between. Instead, he tolerated people in the back of the plane dictating his destinations.

Nonetheless, flying time was flying time.

He'd take it.

He typed in Le Bon Temps Roule. Scowled at his phone. That couldn't be right. The bar was across town, near the zoo. The hotel was in the French Quarter close to Jackson Square.

Within walking distance from where he stood. There must two bars with the same name.

Instead, he put in the hotel. Only about a ten minute walk from here. Without the crowds, he would have no problem getting back there.

He walked downstairs and went out onto the street. The weather could not have been more perfect. The sky was clear. Not a cloud to be seen. Perfect flying weather.

He stopped by Café Du Monde, ordered coffee and a beignet. There were mostly families out this early and couples. He caught himself searching for his sister. His head told him she wouldn't be here, but his heart never stopped searching. He'd given up on fighting that a long time ago. Now it was just something he did.

Would most likely always be a part of him.

The coffee was hot and the beignet was sweet. He couldn't ask for anything more.

The hotel was a straight walk down St. Ann Street. There would be no getting lost this time. The street vendors were setting up as he walked past Jackson Square.

Perhaps he would come back later and see what the local artists had to offer. Since he didn't come to the city often, he might as well take advantage of it.

He had a flight scheduled to Chicago next week for a regular client. An older businessman this time. Completely different kind of experience.

Just as he had last night, he walked past the front door to the Place d'Armes hotel. Stopped in front of the first tall oak door.

Pushed on the panel.

It didn't budge.

Where was the name of the bar?

The door was smooth – no plaque. Nothing at all on the door.

He stepped back into the street. There were several tall oak panels, but none of them appeared to be working doors. He pushed on each one, just to be sure. Searched for hinges, doorknobs, something.

I must look like an idiot.

One hand on his waist, the other on his forehead, he tried to remember the events from last night. Had he really had too much to drink?

Surely one drink wouldn't leave him this disoriented.

Not afraid to ask for directions, he went into the hotel lobby and waited until the clerk finished checking out a tall brunette female. She smiled as she walked past him, suitcase in tow.

"Checking in?" the young girl behind the desk asked. Her fingernails were painted blue and she had a streak of blue down the left side of her hair.

"No," Bradley shook his head. "I was at a bar last night – the Le Bon Temps Roule. Right next door. I know they're probably closed, but can you point me in the right direction?"

"It's over on… Magazine Street, I think."

"Yeah. I know. I found that one on my map. But I was here, last night, and went inside. There must be two of them."

The girl with the blue nails and the blue streak in her hair laughed. "A lot of people get confused. I promise. There's no bar next door."

Bradley considered. Started to walk away, but turned back. "Ok," he said. "Can I ask your manager, just for my own piece of mind?"

The girl shrugged. "Sure. I'll get him."

She went into the back and a burly man, in perhaps his late thirties, followed her back out. "What can I do for you?" he asked.

Bradley repeated his request.

The man shook his head before Bradley could finish his

question. "I've been working here since I was her age. I
promise. There's never been a bar on this side of the street.
And the only Le Bon Temps Roule is across town – out by the
zoo. Not the best part of town, you know."

"What about here, in the hotel?" Bradley asked, a swirl of
confusion and panic running through him.

The man shook his head. "There is no bar in this hotel."

"Do you have anyone working here by the name of Camille
Lafleur?"

"Lafleur is a common name, but no." The man said, and
started to walk away.

"Wait," Bradley called out, placing a hand on the counter.

"What is it?"

"I don't understand."

The man took a step back toward him. "There are many
possible explanations," he said. Assuming you weren't
somewhere else, perhaps you had too much to drink. Or…" He
glanced at the girl with the blue nails and hair. She shrugged.
"Some say the place is haunted. Perhaps you saw a ghost."

Bradley stepped back, his mind locked. He knew he hadn't
been lost and he had only had one drink. Not even the whole
thing. But the smoke from the cigars had given the room a
haziness. No one had spoken to him other than Camille and
the other barkeeper.

"They say there is a man who talks to people and some have
seen a girl."

Bradley turned and rushed out of the hotel into the street.
He bent over, his hands on his knees. He'd seen a ghost then.
Had a crush on a ghost?

No. She hadn't been a ghost. Ghosts didn't have beautiful
green eyes.

Never. Not in even one ghost story had a ghost ever had
green eyes.

Since he had nothing else to do, he walked back to Jackson Square and went inside the cathedral.

It was cool inside and quiet.

A few tourists were already there, but mostly a handful of people scattered about, praying.

He sat on a bench. Turned his eyes to the front of the church.

He'd ruled out being intoxicated. Being lost. Barring seeing ghosts, there was only one explanation left.

Camille sat at her father's huge desk. Technically, she supposed, it was her desk, since she was the one using it this winter.

She liked it here in the city.

Granted, she didn't like the society balls and such, especially the ones in the summer when the new debutantes came out and all anyone talked about was marriage, but she did like the tavern. Maybe it reminded her of her brothers and the good times they had as children here. At the plantation, they were always out hunting and fishing. Those things hadn't appealed to her. She went occasionally, but only because she liked to ride horseback.

Camille didn't see herself as a typical woman. She liked horses, but not hunting. She didn't care for cooking or traditional feminine tasks. Not that she needed to do those things. Her family had people to do the cooking and cleaning. But she also didn't care for needlepoint or any of the other things her mother did to pass the time. Knitting was tolerable, especially since it was practical and led to things like socks or the new shawl in the trunk of her room.

But Camille liked numbers. She loved numbers, in fact.

She'd taken to bookkeeping like a duck to water. She'd sat

on her father's lap and spout out the answers before he could begin to add the numbers. She was always right.

He had finally given the task over to her. He didn't care so much for it anyway. He preferred to be outside. Riding around the fields. Watching the cotton from seeds to harvest. Or socializing with patrons and vendors.

She quickly tallied the numbers from last night's income. It wasn't that she minded the soirees and the BBQs. She enjoyed the dancing and the conversations with men. What she didn't like, she mused, was the pressure by certain men to marry her and take her away. Camille loved her home – both of them actually. And she would never marry if it meant being taken away from them.

She set her ink pen in the ink well and scowled at the ledger. The only income was from one new membership. She had taken the money herself. The man's name was Edwin McGregor. Edwin was a man in his forties, at least.

There was no record of the young man with the blue eyes and the short brown hair with the perfect white teeth.

She read back through the list of members. She knew each and every one of them. He was most certainly not on the list.

It struck her then that she didn't even know his name.

AFTER LEAVING THE CATHEDRAL, BRADLEY WALKED ALONG THE river walk until the shops opened. Then he went to work. His first purchase from a high end department store was a black wool tuxedo jacket and black bow tie. His next purchase was a little more difficult to find. He must have gone in every shop in the French quarter before he found the perfect black mask. He was so excited he didn't notice until he went to check out that it didn't have attached ties to secure it around his head.

He must have looked as crestfallen as he felt because the girl behind the counter asked him to wait. "Just a minute, hon, I think we have some black ribbon in the back."

A few minutes later, she came back, and secured some ribbon to the mask. She asked him to sit, and secured the mask over his eyes and tied it around his head.

"There," she said, gesturing to a mirror, "what do you think?"

Bradley smiled. "It's perfect."

Keeping his mask on and feeling quite debonair, he ate a late lunch at a quiet outdoor café.

He had walked by the Place d'Armes at least half a dozen times. Still no door to a bar.

Ian called to confirm tomorrow's flight to Houston. They would meet in the hotel lobby at 10:00 am. Bradley suspected that an afternoon flight would have been more to their liking, but he would be ready. That meant no alcohol for him tonight. His personal philosophy was no alcohol twenty-four hours before a flight. It made him sluggish. And being sluggish in the air was not a good thing.

During his walk on the river's edge it had occurred to him that perhaps he needed to recreate last night's events.

Only tonight, he planned to start much earlier.

If his theory was correct, everything had to be just right.

CHAPTER 2

*C*amille took her time getting dressed for her evening shift to serve at the tavern. She'd taken an afternoon nap, so she was prepared to work as late as her father would permit. He was planning to play cards tonight, so hopefully he would forget about her, or at least allow her to stay later since she would be within his eyesight.

She put on one of her favorite gowns – a deep lilac, with lots of layers and a bow at the right side of the bodice. Brushing her hair, her thoughts wandered to the man she hoped to see tonight. It was too much to hope that he would come back. The city was rife with tourists right now with Mardi Gras. He'd said he wasn't from here. Perhaps he'd just been passing through.

Or, her heart surged with hope, as she tied her white mask over her eyes, he was staying for the celebration. In that case, he may wander back into her tavern.

This time, she vowed, she would find out more about him. Beginning, at least, with his name.

Satisfied with her appearance after checking the mirror, she left her room and went down the hallway, down the stairway, to the family dining area. She loved the way that this

townhouse was set up. The building had three stories, well...
four if counting the attic. The bottom floor was the tavern –
customer area with lots of tables, a serving counter, then a
whole kitchen and storage area dedicated to the tavern behind
that. There was also an office where her father spent much of
his time during the day meeting with other men. The second
floor was the living area – a parlor, kitchen, and dining area.
There was also a library and another office where the actual
work took place. That's where Camille spent her days.

The third floor was dedicated to bedrooms. Two of the
bedrooms had little sitting areas. One of those bedrooms was
Camille's. The other was her mother's. Her mother had the
largest bedroom and, besides having a sitting area, it was
connected to her father's bedroom. The other two bedrooms
belonged to her brothers.

It had been incredibly quiet and lonely since her brothers
left. She missed them terribly.

She wandered into the family dining area where there was
always food available.

"What would you like to eat Miss Camille?" Abby, the
servant in charge of the dining room asked as Camille entered
the room.

"Just something light."

"A cheese and fruit tray?"

"Yes," Camille agree, "That would be perfect." She sat at the
large dining table and Abby went to get the food.

Camille hardly had time to sit before her father came into
the room.

"Good afternoon, my dear," he said, coming to give his
daughter a quick peck on the cheek.

"How are you Father?" Camille worried about her father.
Perhaps overly much. "Are you prepared for your card game?"

Her father sat at the table across from her. "I am indeed. My
opponents don't stand a chance."

"That's good to hear. Thank you for letting me work in the tavern this weekend."

"It baffles me, Camille, why you enjoy it so much."

"Perhaps I take after you," she said, a teasing note in her voice.

Her father merely grunted.

Camille knew that her father also disliked the Mardi Gras balls. He would make an appearance with her mother when she was in town, of course, then return to the tavern to play cards later into the night.

"Any new members last night?" he asked.

"Two," she answered. Though, truth be told, only one had paid. As soon as she learned his name, she would add her mysterious man to the list of paid members.

After much consideration, she had determined that he was not a man of means; hence she didn't think he would have the hefty sum available required to become a member of her father's elite club.

Besides, she blamed herself for coming up with the idea. Unless her father planned to keep the membership low, Camille had decided the whole membership thing was a bad idea after all.

"You look festive," her father commented. "Are you certain you wouldn't rather go to the ball? If you do, I'll forego my card game and accompany you."

"I wouldn't dream of keeping you from your card game, Father. I know how much you enjoy it."

Abby appeared with Camille's cheese tray and offered to bring something for Mr. Lafleur. Her father declined, but Camille knew that he would eat later with his business associates.

"If you need anything while I'm out," he said, "Billy will be here."

Camille smiled. Billy was the largest man she knew. He

usually stood somewhere within view when she was in the tavern.

"I'm not worried, Father."

He stood up, pushed his chair beneath the table. Camille was proud of her father. He was a handsome man. Sturdily built, but trim, nonetheless. And he always kept his mustache trimmed and his hair short.

"I'm not sure if your ability to not worry about things is one of your best qualities or your worst," he said. "I'll see you downstairs."

Perhaps her best quality was not letting her father know that she did, indeed, worry. But her worry was confined to her family. Her father. Her mother. Her brothers. She worried not about things like marriage or men fighting in the tavern.

She finished her fruit and cheese, then went downstairs and began preparing for the evening. Made sure all the most requested liquors were well-stocked.

Satisfied that she was ready for the evening, she retrieved a novel from her father's office and sat at one of the tables to wait for the first customers. She was reading The Last of the Mohicans. It was her third time to read it, but each time, she learned something new.

Engrossed in her book, she didn't hear the door open.

She nearly toppled out of her chair, however, when someone pulled out the chair next to her.

It was him!

And he was grinning from ear to ear.

BRADLEY BEGAN WALKING AT FIVE O'CLOCK. IT WASN'T YET DARK, but he didn't want to risk missing a single minute with Camille – whether she was ghost or spirit or even of his imagination.

His scientific mind had come to the conclusion that he needed to start by waiting until nightfall, perhaps even when the streets were crowded. Part of the whole recreation process. He began walking a route that would take him down the sidewalk in front of the Place d'Armes hotel. He walked slowly around the block. Each time, it was a little more crowded. He truly hoped this worked, especially before he began to step on people again. The smell of alcohol already floated in the air.

Fortunately, the pleasant weather had held. He didn't relish the thought of perspiring in his new tuxedo jacket. Or having to wear it drenched from another rain storm.

His fifth time around the block, the sun dipped below the Mississippi River and a cold breeze drifted through the air. No one else seemed to notice. He was almost to the hotel. He hopped onto the sidewalk and put his hands in his pockets. The drunken reverie had resumed around him.

He passed the hotel and...

There.

There was the Le Bon Temps Roule door. He took out his phone and snapped a picture of the sign. Then as an afterthought, stepped back and snapped a picture with both the hotel and the bar sign. It took a minute to get a shot between tourists.

But now he had something to show them. He had not been lost. He locked his phone and slipped it back into his pocket.

He pushed the heavy wooden door open. Unlike last night, there was no smoke yet. Hence, he had a clear view of the room.

The bar was to the left as he'd remembered and tables were scattered around the room. Only now they were empty.

With one exception.

He recognized her immediately. Today she wore a purple dress with her white mask. Her eyes glued to a book, she didn't even hear him come into the room.

A woman after his own heart, indeed.

As a pilot, Bradley used his time spent waiting, of which there was lots of, reading.

His mother accused him of using reading to escape reality.

He could think of no better means of escape.

But at the moment, all he knew was that he had found her.

Stepping to the table, he pulled out the chair next to hers and she jumped, nearly dropping her book.

He grinned at her. Somehow his catching her off-guard made her seem more… real.

"You scared me half to death," she said.

"I apologize," he said, though his elation at seeing her overshadowed any regret at startling her. "May I?" he asked, indicating the chair.

"Of course," she said, seeming to shake off her surprise. "Can I get you something to drink?"

He almost said yes. He wanted anything she offered. But caught himself. "I can't drink tonight."

She looked askance at him. "But you're in a tavern."

"I know," he said, "What can I say?"

"It's because you had too much last night," she said.

He nodded slowly. That was a good enough explanation. For the time-being. Right now he wanted to know about her.

"What's your name?" she asked.

He raised an eyebrow. And perhaps she wanted to know about him.

"I need to add you to the list of members," she added quickly.

"Bradley Becquerel," he told her. "But I haven't paid my membership. Do you take credit?"

That elicited an odd expression on her face. "I took care of it."

"I can pay," he put a hand in his pocket to pull out his money clip.

She touched his other arm lightly on his sleeve. "We don't take credit anyway, so truly, don't worry about it."

He left it alone. The pressure of her hand on his arm, even through his jacket, was enough to keep him from arguing.

"What are you reading?" he asked.

She glanced at the book, as though she had forgotten it. "The Last of the Mohicans."

"Oh. That was a good one."

"You read it?" she asked, her eyes lit up.

"It was required in English lit, but I liked it. My sister especially liked Daniel Day-Lewis," he said, absorbing the pang of grief that went with mentioning his sister.

Camille frowned at the book. "I haven't gotten to that part yet."

"Hmm."

The door opened and a couple of men came in.

"I think that's my cue to go to work," she said, standing up.

"Oh," Bradley didn't try to hide his disappointment. "Is it ok if I stay?"

She smiled at him. "I'd like that. Stay here so I can come talk to you in between customers."

He returned her smile. And watched as she went to work.

She moved in the costume as though it was second nature.

She served the two men drinks, then true to her word, came to stand in front of him, a glass of water in tow.

"Have you worked here long?" he asked.

"No. This is my first season."

"You seem to be good at it."

"I practically grew up here. My brothers and I spent a lot of time here during the summers growing up."

"As children? Here?"

She laughed. And he was mesmerized.

"During the daytime," she clarified.

"Then your family… owns it?"

She nodded. "I'll be right back."

He hadn't heard anyone call her. Maybe he'd asked too much too soon.

If her family owned the bar, that certainly explained a lot. She looked more like a guest than an employee. Even in costume, she looked as though she were going to a gala instead of to work. Perhaps it was the way she carried herself. Her self-assurance.

A few minutes later, she came back and sat down next to him. She laced her fingers beneath her chin. Again, he longed to see her face beneath the mask.

"Tell me about you," she said.

"I'd rather talk about you," he said.

"You have new clothes."

She'd noticed. He beamed. "I do. I apologize for being so underdressed last night. I just sort of wandered in."

She smiled. "It's a good thing you had too much."

He laughed. He loved it that they already had a private joke. "Do you always dress up or is it because of Mardi Gras?"

"I'm not really dressed up," she said, running a hand over her hair.

"You know…" he said. "It doesn't really seem fair."

"What doesn't seem fair?"

"It doesn't seem fair that you've seen me without my mask, but I haven't seen you without yours."

Her lips curved into a bow, but she shook her head. "I can't," she said.

"It doesn't come off?" he asked, leaning forward. "Is it tattooed on there?" He reached out to touch her mask.

She slapped his hand down. "No! It's not tattooed. Of course it comes off."

"Then why?"

"I promised my father."

Bradley leaned back. "Your father is a wise man."

She smiled, pride evident in her face.

The door opened and another group of men came into the door. "My cue," she said, standing up, "to go to work."

He watched her movements behind the bar. She smiled and chatted with the men as she took their orders. One of them addressed her as Miss Lafleur. Perhaps her father only thought the mask served the purpose of keeping her in disguise. Nonetheless, their comments were respectful.

He picked up the book she was reading, flipped through the pages. The book felt new and was in excellent condition.

His gaze turned back to Camille. She sent a quick smile in his direction as she opened a bottle of wine.

Her smile sent a tingle through him down to his toes. And put a smile on his lips.

He flipped open the front cover of the book. There was writing on the first page.

For Camille Lafleur,

All my best,

J. Fennimore Cooper

May 1834

Bradley's thoughts twisted and collided upon themselves. He was still staring at the autograph when Camille came back and sat in front of him.

"Where did you get this?" he whispered, his voice unsteady.

"My father got it for me when he went to New York a few years ago."

"It has your name in it."

"Sure. My father asked him to sign it for me."

"Your father knows him." His voice was barely audible.

"I think they met. Why? What's wrong?"

Bradley looked up into her eyes. "This book was signed a few years ago?" he repeated.

She nodded. "Yes," She turned the book toward her. "1834."

"He signed it to you."

She nodded. Shrugged.

Bradley grabbed the edge of the table with both his hands.

His theory had been right.

It was true.

CAMILLE'S GAZE DARTED AROUND THE ROOM, THEN BACK TO Bradley's face. He looked as though he might be ill.

She took his arm to get his attention. "Are you well?"

He lifted his gaze to her. His expression looked like... the time her brother swore up and down he'd seen a young girl jump off the balcony of his room. In this very house. Of course, he'd been twelve.

He didn't answer. Instead, he reached out and put a hand lightly on her cheek.

She shivered. And closed her eyes.

Then he took her hands in his and squeezed. He squeezed until she opened her eyes and looked into his. "I..." he began, then stopped, glanced away, then reclaimed her gaze. "I need to ask you something and it's very very important."

She nodded.

"What is today's date?"

"March 2."

"Good," he said, "But what is the year?"

"1838."

He closed his eyes. Opened them again, searching her face for... something. Then he took a deep breath. "I know you're doing the costume thing and all. But I mean the real and true year."

He was daft. "1838," she said again.

He released her hand and leaned back in the chair. Scrubbed his hands over his face. "Who's the president?" he asked.

"Martin Van Buren," she said easily. "He was elected last year. Normally I wouldn't keep up with such things... but..."

Bradley was laughing. He was laughing so hard, his eyes were moist.

Camille glanced around to make sure they weren't being watched. Had he escaped from the insane asylum?

The one time she takes someone under wing, he turns out to be insane.

He sobered. Wiped his eyes. "I'm sorry," he said. "It's just so... outlandish."

She scowled at him.

"I think I'll take that drink after all."

BRADLEY HAD BELIEVED HIS SISTER, ERIKA. TRULY HE HAD.

He had spent countless hours contemplating the possibilities of time-travel.

He had even entertained the possibility that Camille was in the past – especially after he had been unable to find the bar during the day. Hell, he'd even bought a tux and a mask in order to try and blend in just in case he was able to step back through that door.

But now...

Now that he had actually stepped back through that door... And was looking at the possibility that Camille did, indeed, live one hundred eighty years in the past...

His world was turned upside down.

He needed to talk to Erika. He needed to talk to his sister.

"Here's your whiskey," Camille said, setting a glass on the table in front of him.

"Thank you," he said, automatically, but only stared at it.

I have to fly tomorrow.

What if he couldn't get back?

His sister had traveled into the past and, as far as he knew, she had only been able to return one or two times. To the best of his knowledge, she was here. In the past. Now.

His heart tripped up a notch at the possibility of seeing her again. For all intents and purposes, she had been dead to him for the past year.

Another group of men just walked into the bar. There was a card game going and tonight's group seemed louder than last night's.

What would happen when he walked out that door?

Would he go back to life as he knew it or would he walk out into a 19th century world? That thought sent a wave a panic through him. An airplane pilot in the 1800s. Would be a little difficult to find a job.

"You aren't going to drink that, are you?" Camille asked.

Bradley returned his gaze to Camille's green eyes. He'd worked all day just to see her again and here he was going down a rabbit hole.

He reached out, placed his hand over hers. "I apologize profusely. Please forgive me."

She flushed.

Bradley remembered, too late, that he'd probably just committed a faux pas just by touching her. He jerked his hand back. Brushed it through his hair.

Sighed.

But whatever may be, this was the girl he could not take his eyes from for more than a few seconds. He'd only had this butterfly in the stomach feeling one other time in his life. It was in third grade during a summer camp. It had been a camp for boys, but there were two college girls doing volunteer work during the days. Their job was to teach the boys manners – things like how to pull out a chair for a girl or how to walk on the outside of the sidewalk. Bradley had never even spoken to her as far as he could remember. He'd just nodded mutely as she had gently taken his arm and changed sides on the sidewalk.

Savannah Richards.

She had been the woman of his dreams throughout his adolescent years. The crush had faded, of course. And he had never seen her again.

But that feeling was one he had never completely forgotten. He had just never had it happen again.

Until yesterday.

Camille Lafleur was his new Savannah Richards.

Only this time, he was old enough to do something about it.

He smiled what must have been a rather wolfish grin because her eyes widened.

"Tell me something about you," he said.

She tore her gaze from his, a flush spreading over her cheeks. "There's nothing to tell."

"Do you have any brothers and sisters?" he asked. He wanted to know anything. Everything.

She nodded. "I have two brothers. But they are in Texas fighting Comanches."

"Comanches?"

"Indians."

"Yes, I've heard of them." *I've just never heard of anyone fighting them.* Only in the movies. "You must worry about them."

She sighed. "I worry about them all the time."

"It's hard when you're the one left behind," he said, again thinking of his sister. And the fleeting thought that perhaps, just perhaps he could see her again.

Her eyes grew misty with unshed tears. "I wanted to go with them, but they refused to let me. When I threatened to follow them, my older brother made me promise not to. He said if he was worried about me, he'd probably not pay attention and get himself killed."

"I can only image that was enough to keep you here. It would be enough for me."

"It was," she whispered. A tear slid from her right eye. She had her back to the room. No one was watching them.

Bradley leaned forward and caught the tear with his finger. Then he swept a finger beneath her mask at her hairline near her ear.

Her breathe hitched.

"Maybe…" he said. "Maybe you should take this thing off for a little while."

She didn't move. Almost seemed to be holding her breath as they gazed into each other's eyes.

She nodded. Perhaps he imagined it, but it was enough. Before she could change her mind, he swept the mask over her head.

Any thoughts he may have been having came to a dead stop.

He wanted to devour her. Right then and there.

Camille was the most gorgeous female he had ever seen. Her features were perfectly delicate. Her skin flawless.

He put a hand back on her cheek. Soft. That was the only coherent thought that registered in his befuddled brain.

He swayed toward her. They were inches apart now. Her lips were parted.

There was movement behind her.

Though every cell in his body protested, he whispered, "You'd better put this back on."

She didn't move.

"Hurry," he said.

Spurred into action, she put her mask back on as someone called her name.

"My father," she murmured.

A stab of fear shot through Bradley's heart.

It was only a mask. He swallowed a bubble of laughter. He felt like he'd violated her. But it was only a mask.

Now he could see why her father insisted she wear it while she worked in the bar. Or as she called it, the tavern.

CAMILLE'S FEET WERE FROZEN IN PLACE. HER FATHER WAS A reasonable man. Mostly.

But at the moment, he was being most unreasonable.

Camille, as the accountant of the tavern, had determined to waive Bradley's membership fee. Could her father just override her like this? He could, of course, since he was the owner, but must she allow him to?

"Your name is not on the roster, Sir," her father was standing toe to toe with Bradley. They appeared to be evenly matched in height and stature.

"I apologize," Bradley said, "I only just recently learned of the membership fee. Your daughter was very kind to not pressure me on the matter."

"My daughter doesn't worry herself overly much with money."

Surely her father jested. She prided herself on keeping very accurate books.

Her father must have seen the shock and insult on her face. "She allows the kindness of her heart to take precedence," he added quickly.

"I can assure you that I'm good for the money," Bradley said.

Her father was partially right. Camille's heart broke for him. He obviously didn't have money. His clothes were embarrassingly out of style. Where did he even find such things to wear? Even his shoes had no heels.

"Very well, then," her father said, glancing between the two of them. "I'm sure my daughter had a good reason for making an exception. I will trust her judgment. However, I must ask that you bring the funds – twenty dollars - with you when you come back into the tavern.

"Of course," Bradley said.

"It's settled then," her father said, turning away and, as they watched, chose a table and joined a card game.

"I'm so sorry," Camille said, quietly, so only Bradley could hear.

"No. He's right. There should be no exception made for me," he turned his head to meet her gaze.

Her heart fluttered. For a moment, before her father walked up, she'd thought he was going to kiss her. He'd boldly removed her mask, touched her face, and… she had been going to allow the kiss. In fact, she wanted the kiss.

Even now, she longed to remove their masks again and perhaps he would be inclined to try to kiss her again.

She chastised herself at the thought. Her father was there, watching them. If her father saw Bradley kiss her, he would probably challenge him to a duel and one of them would die. That could certainly not be allowed to happen.

She loved her father, despite her current annoyance with him. And Bradley, well… she certainly didn't want to lose him.

"I should go," Bradley said.

She shook her head. She didn't want him to go.

"I don't want to anger your father."

"Will you come back?" she asked softly, holding her breath, waiting for his response.

"Yes," he said, staring deeply into her eyes. "I will do everything in my power to come back."

She nodded. Bit her lower lip.

"If I don't come back, know that…" He raised a hand, then seemed to think better of touching her. "Know that it was not from a lack of trying."

He held out his hand and she placed hers in his. He pressed his lips against her skin, sending shivers up and down her spine.

"I will see you, ma chère."

He released her hand, and, turning, walked away from her.

She watched as Bradley neared the door. Only a few steps more, and he would disappear into the night. She may never see him again.

That thought left her with a hollow ache and he wasn't even out of her sight yet.

She needed to tell him… something… though she knew not what.

Suddenly spurred into action, she picked up her skirts and raced through the room, dodging tables, and chairs.

Earl Harps stepped out in front of her. "Excuse me, Sir," she said, putting a hand on his arm to practically shove him aside.

"Is there a fire?" he asked, with a loud laugh, still blocking her path.

"No," she said, turning and taking a different route. She had no time for banter.

It was difficult to see in the smoke, but she kept her eyes on Bradley.

As he reached out to touch the door, she called his name.

She was three feet from him now.

He turned back as his hand pushed the door open, and he stepped through.

She slowed as her eyes met his. He raised a hand to reach for her.

With their gazes locked, he vanished.

CHAPTER 3

Camille was still moving forward. She grasped the door with one hand and reached out with the other. However, her hand swept through nothing but air.

She stepped out into the cool night air. The cool, clear night air. Without the cigar smoke, she had a clear view up and down the street. Other than a horse and buggy making its way through the mud on the other side of the street, the street was deserted.

She slumped against the open door.

Her mind blank.

Then racing. What was this?

A ghost?

Her heart hitched.

A figment of her imagination?

But no... her father had seen him, too. Her gaze shot back to her father, leaning back in his chair, laughing with his friends, completely unaware that her life was coming apart at the seams.

She certainly couldn't tell her father about this. He would think her daft, or worse, put her in the insane asylum.

Either way, he would not believe her. He would say *I told you not to talk to strange men.*

And he would no longer allow her to work in the tavern.

That thought alone was enough to shut down the idea of telling her father about Bradley's sudden evaporation.

"Camille," her father called, standing behind her.

She jumped.

"What are you doing?"

"Nothing, Father." She kept her eyes down. He could too easily see right through her.

"Your young man left?"

Her gaze lifted to his. "You all but told him to go away."

"I'm sorry, My Pet. I didn't realize how much it meant to you that he stay."

"It's too late now," she said, feeling the tears well in her eyes.

"Nonsense," he said. "He'll be back."

"I don't think you understand, Father." Her chin trembled.

"I saw the way he looked at you. He'll be back alright. I just hope you want to see him again."

She wanted him to come back more than anything in the world. But a man who vanished into thin air may have some difficulties doing so.

"David is here," her father was saying. "Perhaps you need to go upstairs and get some sleep."

Sleep. That was the last thing she wanted to do. She did, however, need some time to think.

Bradley had been there. He had been real. Her father had spoken to him, too.

And he had touched her.

Bradley Becquerel may be a ghost, but he was real to her.

BRADLEY TUNED OUT THE MISERABLE MOANS OF HIS PASSENGERS and completed his pre-flight checklist. There was nothing fun about a hangover. He'd suffered through one, maybe two, during college and had vowed never again. Two drinks and he was done. He'd read a study that said after one drink people looked more attractive – their skin glowed, then after a couple more, the effect diminished, but others started to look more attractive.

Anyway, today's task was to get his clients to Houston, then get back to New Orleans. He'd made a reservation at the Place d'Armes for three nights starting tonight. He had to do laundry and repack his suitcase. What did one pack for a trip into the past?

Most would say he had become insane.

But Bradley Becquerel had never been one to conform to conventional standards.

Whether it put him in the insane category or not, he was going to have another go at it.

He'd met Camille Lafluer for a reason. There was no one in his time he'd ever had that kind of attraction to. He'd tried the whole match.com, tinder swipes, speed dating, and other things he couldn't even remember. He'd gotten a couple of sparks, but nothing worth more than a distant memory.

Perhaps it was something in his genes. Perhaps, he mused he was destined to fall in love with someone from the past.

As he waited for his turn to taxi down the runway, he opened his iPad and began a google search for 1830s currency. He couldn't just take twenty dollars from his money clip and hand it over to the guy.

After a few tangents, he found a notice posted on a website that the City Bank of New Orleans would consider buying old money. If they bought old money, perhaps they had some to sell. Or at least could point him toward a collector who might be willing to part with some collector's notes.

He took a deep steading breath as he answered the voice in his ear giving him the all-clear for take-off. Unfortunately, the bank was closed on Sunday, but he would be there at their door first thing in the morning.

It was early-afternoon before he had his passengers dropped off and his plane squared away. He had to reserve a different plane for the return trip because this one was already spoken for starting tomorrow.

He pulled up at his condo and turned off the motor. He'd never really felt at home here. He knew part of it was missing his sister. She'd helped him pick it out, but she hadn't been around to help him furnish it. He'd brought her furniture here instead.

His return flight was scheduled for seven o'clock, so he had five hours to get everything done and get back to the airport.

After throwing his dirty clothes in the washer, and laying his three nice suits on the bed, he sat down at his desk, pulled out a legal pad, and began writing a letter. It gave him a creepy feeling, but he'd been putting off making out a will, so this served the purpose of spurring him into taking care of that. Or so he tried to convince himself.

His wastebasket was soon overflowing with rejected pages.

Finally, content with his letter, he carefully folded it and placing it in an envelope, laid it in the middle of his desk. He wrote *If you can't find me...* across the front. And what he was left with was a terrible sense of guilt. Who would find it? His grandfather? His mother? The police?

I'm sure I'll be back. I'm just being dramatic.

He checked his watch and tossed his clothes in the dryer. He'd worry about that later. The letter was there... just in case

Taking his phone out of his back pocket, he clicked the home key and gazed at his new wallpaper. Although he hadn't had phone service in the bar, his camera did work. He'd snapped a picture of Camille while she'd been standing at the counter, pouring a drink for someone else. The image was hazy, from the cigar smoke, but he'd zoomed in enough to have an image of her face.

Her image was burned into his memory, but the picture was a reminder that she was, indeed, real.

He packed enough clothes for a week into his suitcase, even though he only planned to be gone for three days, and put his suitcase in the trunk of his Pathfinder SUV.

He checked his watch again. He had a little time left. He threw everything perishable from his refrigerator and hauled it all out to the trash dump. He went online and paid all his bills for the next month.

By that point, he was running late, but still made it to the airport on time. Not that the plane was going anywhere without him.

Turns out the plane wasn't going anywhere with him. It needed a part for the engine and would be delayed until morning.

CAMILLE TAPPED HER FINGERS AGAINST THE COUNTER AND scowled at the door. Marcus would be coming to get her at any moment. The clock would soon be tolling the ten o'clock hour and it wasn't proper for her to be here into the night hours. Her father was already allowing her to push the limits.

I don't want you to get the reputation of being a bar maid, he'd told her that morning. Her reputation was the last thing she cared about at the moment, but her father was right, of course. Her father was always right. Almost always.

Bradley wasn't coming tonight.

Her father had assured her that he would, but there had been no sign of him.

He'd been a fleeting ghost into her life.

Her imagination had been active all day. Perhaps he'd recently been killed and was merely passing through on his way to Heaven. Camille didn't believe in ghosts, but she didn't disbelieve in them either. If she determined that Bradley had been a ghost, then she supposed she did believe after all.

She believed in Bradley.

"Miss Camille," Marcus said, at her elbow.

She nodded. "I'm coming."

"Are you well, Miss?"

She shook her head. "I don't know Marcus."

"You feel ill?"

"Yes," she said. *My heart aches.*

"You take care of yourself, Miss."

Camille picked up her skirts. "Thank you Marcus," she said, but didn't bother to look up. She'd run out of fake smiles for the evening.

She went straight upstairs to her room and, after lighting a candle, unbuttoned her bodice, and stepped out of her dress. She put on her nightgown, and went to stand in front of the open window, enjoying the fresh air. She had a perfect view of the street below. She watched a few people walking to and fro. But no sign of Bradley here either.

Her heart heavy, she climbed into bed, and curled beneath the blankets.

Her world had been turned upside down.

By the ghost of a man.

BRADLEY LANDED AT THE NEW ORLEANS AIRPORT AT TEN Monday morning. He took a taxi to the French quarter and checked into the Place d'Armes to drop off his luggage. He then set out to the City Bank of New Orleans.

The representative didn't seem overly surprised at his request. He specialized in rare currency. And, even though he didn't have any 1830's money in the bank, he made a phone call and set up a meeting with a private collector.

By 2:00, Bradley was the proud owner of one twenty-dollar bill in currency dated 1831 and five other hundred dollar bills dated in the early 1830s – just in case. The money was large – much larger than modern-day money and he found the intricate designs quite pretty. He carefully folded them and shoved them into his pocket, thankful the rare bills hadn't broken his bank account.

Since he'd missed a night, he was uncertain that the door would even be there again. After his sister told him about her time-travel experience, he'd spent some time researching different theories about it. Of course, the mainstream culture thought it was merely fodder for media and anyone who truly believed would be put in the insane asylum.

But. In the time-travel subculture, there were tons of theories. Involving everything to the clothes a person wore to the movement of the moon.

Obsession. That was the only word he had to describe his need to see Camille again.

He had been staring into her eyes when he had walked through that door. He'd held out his hand to her and she to him. Then one of them had disappeared.

Since the door to the bar was the tangible thing he'd walked through, he could only surmise that it was a portal of some type. He must have been the one to disappear because he'd been the one who walked through the door.

What must she think?

Bradley had the advantage, he thought, due to his sister and the Internet. And even armed with that little bit of information, he was confused and bewildered. She must be ten times so.

He sat in a small café with a view of the Mississippi River, watching the barges traveling back and forth.

Would the door be there tonight?

Along with that question, another stray thought kept

swirling in his mind. What if it closed while he was on the other side?

The thought surfaced, then swirled out of sight again.

He couldn't let his mind go down that path.

Right now, his only focus was on seeing Camille again.

CHAPTER 4

*T*he next evening, it was with a heavy heart that Camille chose a silver gown for the evening.

She wouldn't see Bradley again, she told herself for the thousandth time.

He had been nothing more than a fleeting visitor. A lost soul on his way to Heaven.

Camille wasn't overly religious, but she had a good Catholic foundation. Enough that she believed in the afterlife.

Perhaps even more so now that she had witnessed a strange otherworldly occurrence.

Her ghostly encounter had strong hands and clear blue eyes.

And… different clothing. One night a plain white shirt and the second a more formal coat… and a mask.

The memory of his fingertips against her cheek sent a shiver down her spine. She brushed her hair, leaving it long and softly curled tonight.

Then she tied a matching silver mask over her eyes. Only one more night and she would be free of the mask. But did it matter?

Her heart wasn't in it tonight. After last night's

disappointment at not seeing Bradley, she would have preferred to curl up with a book and stay to herself.

Alas, she had too much invested in convincing her father that she should be allowed to work behind the bar in the tavern. Lifting her chin, she made her way downstairs and greeted Marcus with a smile.

"Afternoon, Miss," he said. "There's a party coming in early tonight after the parade."

"Parade?" She vaguely remembered reading about a parade in the paper, but hadn't considered that it might affect their business.

"That's right. Your father is opening the tavern up to the public."

"Is that so?" she asked, not bothering to hide the sarcasm from her voice. After all the grief he'd given Bradley over paying his membership fee, now just anyone could come in! Her father would most definitely be hearing about this.

Nonetheless, she barely had time to check her stock before the tourists started pouring in. Juggling the wine orders with the whiskey orders kept her hopping. The customers were a mixture of both men and women tonight – different than the usual all male clientele. Such was the way of Mardi Gras.

It was all about breaking conventions. As long as one wore their mask, she added wryly.

Though her head told her it was fruitless, her heart continued to search for any sign of Bradley.

As a second wave of customers came into the already crowded tavern, David appeared at her elbow and offered to give her a break.

"I would love to take a break," she said, gladly handing over the responsibility of the work, even if only for a few minutes.

She went to the back office and sat at the desk. The mask she wore tonight was causing her skin to itch, so she reached up and removed it. After dropping the mask on the desk, she ran her hand through her hair, fluffing it up.

One hand tangled in her hair, she began making some notes on a piece of paper. She would have lots to do tomorrow with the cash flow from tonight.

At the sound of footsteps, she looked up expecting to see Marcus coming to bring her back to work.

Instead, she dropped the ink pen on the paper, sending ink all over the paper and desk.

Bradley stood leaning against the door jamb watching her. How long had he been there?

Again, she was struck that his clothes were a little odd, but he smiled at her and her focus moved back to his face.

"Good evening," he said.

She stood up, shoving her chair back in the process, and, stepping around it, took two steps back, the desk between them.

Concern on his face, he stood up straight, but made no move toward her. "I'm sorry. I didn't mean to frighten you."

"I'm not frightened," she said, but she was. Her heart tripped in her chest, her body tense. Was she afraid because she thought he might be a ghost? Or was she afraid because of the effect he had on her?

"The man up front said I could come back here to pay you," Bradley said, reaching into his pocket and pulling out a crumpled note. Moving slowly, he stepped forward to lay it on the center of the desk.

Keeping her eyes glued to his, she stepped back again, but bumped up against the wall.

He moved a step back again and smiled.

She swallowed thickly and took a deep, ragged breath.

Her gaze darted toward her mask. Then back to his eyes. It was odd how she felt exposed without her mask. It wasn't like she'd ever worn a mask before three days ago.

Perhaps it was the way his eyes seemed to devour her.

Suddenly, he reached up and stripped his own mask from his face.

She gasped.

His smile had turned wolfish again.

Her palms pressed against the smooth wood of the wall behind her. There was no where else to go.

He took a step forward.

She tore her gaze from his. "He's a ghost," she said softly.

Bradley froze. Scowled. "Miss Lafleur," he said. "Look at me."

She did as he asked, the way he said her name made her toes tingle.

"I'm not a ghost."

"How do I know?"

"Have you ever seen a ghost?"

"No."

"Have you ever spoken to a ghost?"

She shook her head.

"Then don't you think it's likely I'm not a ghost either?"

She shrugged.

"I could just as easily think you're a ghost."

"Me?" Her eyes widened. What an odd thing to say. She looked down at herself. Shook her head as she looked back up. Ran a hand along her arms.

"Do you believe that you could touch a ghost?" he persisted.

"No. Ghosts are impalpable."

He nodded. "We agree on that, then."

She nodded.

"Shall we test it?"

"How are we going to do that?" she asked.

"Well... unless we're both ghosts, which I think is almost impossible, we shouldn't be able to touch each other."

Camille supposed that the idea of them both being ghosts

was actually a possibility, but highly unlikely. She decided to keep that to herself.

As she considered these possibilities, Marcus came to the door. "Mistress Camille?"

"Yes," she answered.

"Is everything all right?" He asked, looking from one to the other of them.

"Thank you Marcus. Everything is fine."

Marcus took her at her word and left her there.

"Take my hand," Bradley said.

She shook her head imperceptibly.

"You know I'm not a ghost," he said.

She nodded.

"Yet you're still afraid of me."

She pushed off the wall and walked toward him, around the desk. She put out her hand and he grabbed hold of it.

He was the antithesis of intangible.

A look of satisfaction crossed his features.

Now what? She pulled back, but he held tight.

"We can agree that neither one of us is a ghost?"

She nodded. "Yes. But..."

"But?"

"You disappeared. I saw you."

"Yeah," he said, pressed his free hand against his forehead. "Perhaps it was a trick of the light."

"No," she insisted. "I followed you through the door and into the street. You were there. Then you weren't."

"You're right," he said. "But it's difficult for me to explain."

"I'm not a simpleton. It you explain it to me, I'm certain I can understand."

He seemed to consider. While he was distracted, she jerked her hand from his, picked up his twenty-dollar bill and shoved it in a desk drawer.

She then sat back down in the chair, rested her hands on the desk and beneath her chin, and watched him expectantly.

He hadn't moved. Rather, he stood scowling at her.

"You're wearing the same expression my father wore when I asked to accompany my brothers to Texas and when I asked to work in the tavern."

"I can commiserate with your father."

She smiled, in spite of herself. "So? How do you explain your trick of the light?"

His expression grew serious. "I don't think I should."

"Why not?"

"Because you'll think I'm an imbecile."

"You're not an imbecile," she said.

He didn't answer. They watched each other for a few more moments.

"I have to get back out front," she said, picking up her mask, and stepping around the desk. He stood between her and the door. "Do you mind?" she asked.

He moved aside. "Wait. Miss Laflueur."

She stopped at the door, turned back, looked questioningly at him.

"I'm from the future," he said.

"Right," she said and swung around, her skirts swirling around her as she slipped the mask over her eyes and marched back to the room filled with smoke. Forcing a smile on her face, she took her place behind the counter.

She was quickly swamped with customers ordering drinks. But as she opened bottles, poured liquors, washed glasses, and laughed with customers, her thoughts were focused on Bradley.

I'm from the future. She was convinced that he wasn't a ghost. That was a relief. The last thing she needed was to have an infatuation with a ghost.

But a man from the future? Was that truly any better?

It would explain his odd clothing. His unusual speech. The way he didn't seem to belong.

Because he didn't.

He wasn't from here.

Here meaning now.

She watched him out of the corner of her eye as he took a seat at the bar between two other men.

She had to think more about this and get more information. She knew someone to ask. But in the meantime, she couldn't remain angry with him. Even now, as he watched her, his eyes had a haunted look.

Perhaps he had not asked to be here.

Consumed with compassion for this man who sent her heart into wildly erratic rhythms, she took a glass of whiskey and set it on the counter in front of him.

THE BAR – TAVERN – WAS PACKED TONIGHT. AND MONEY WAS changing hands. Apparently the whole membership policy had changed since two nights ago.

Bradley picked up the shot of whiskey and downed it. There was no way he would have another minute to talk to Camille in private tonight. The place was packed.

So, he'd traveled all the way back to 1838 just to pay a membership fee that was no longer required.

And watch the most beautiful girl in the world at work.

He sighed.

And knew he would do it all over again.

How many times could he walk through that door? How many times would he be allowed to walk back and forth through the time portal or whatever it was that allowed him to pass through time?

Why here? Why now?

What would happen if he got stuck here?

As always his thoughts froze on that thought and made a detour. Sure, he'd written a note and left it in his apartment in case he didn't return.

But now. Now that he was actually here again, he was struck with the notion that he might never return.

On a sudden impulse, he pulled out his cell phone. But before he swiped it open, he thought better and, leaving his bar stool, found a private area near the back. With his back to the crowd, he swiped open his phone. He had no signal. His phone looked the same as it did thousands of feet in the air. He had a full charge, though, and quickly pulled up the picture of the street outside.

The temptation was strong to step through the door to see what would happen. Before he did that, though, he needed more information. He slipped his phone back in his pocket.

Making his way through the boisterous crowd, he found his barstool had been taken. He was able to angle his way up to the counter where he signaled for Camille.

She poured a drink and set it in front of him. Before she could walk away, he grabbed her wrist. "Wait," he said.

His gesture drew concerned glances from a couple of men. She smiled sweetly and put her other hand over his. "You are welcome, cousin," she said, brightly.

"Can I talk to you?" He murmured.

She nodded and he released her.

Five minutes later, she snagged his gaze and nodded toward the door leading to the back, where he had found her earlier.

"Are you trying to get yourself killed?" she asked, when they were alone in the back office.

"I just needed a moment to talk with you."

She crossed her arms. "I've got about three minutes before either my father or Billy comes looking for me. I'm not sure which one would be worse for you."

He nodded. He would have to be quick then. No beating around the bush.

"Are you married?"

"No," she answered, quickly, scowling at him.

"Are you single?"

"Pardon?"

He shook his head. Wracked his brain for another way to ask. "Are you... spoken for?"

"You mean am I betrothed?"

"Yes! Are you betrothed?"

"No, I'm not."

He nodded. "Good."

"Why are you asking me these questions?"

Why was he asking indeed. "I'd like to court you."

She inhaled sharply. "Court me?"

"Yes. You know. Call on you."

"Why? What are your intentions?"

"Intentions?" This was truly like speaking a foreign language. "I don't know."

"You don't know."

"No. I'd just like to get to know you better."

She scoffed. "Then no. You may not call on me."

He was speechless. Was this how a woman of 1838 indicated a lack of interest in a man? "What can I do to... I don't know. Spend time with you." *Date you.*

"Before you can spend time with me," she said, "you have to tell me what your intentions are."

"How do I know what my intentions are until I've spent time with you?"

"Surely you don't think I'm simple. A man knows what his intentions are the moment he meets a woman."

As bizarre as that sounded to his ears, he knew she was right. He couldn't name a single man in his social circle who hadn't known the woman he was going to marry on sight. The guy might not have realized he knew it, but he certainly knew if she was someone he merely wanted to dally with. Women were different. Some fell in love at first sight. Others took time to fall in love.

Bradley wasn't sure what he was going to do with Camille Lafleur, but he did know he wanted more than a mere dalliance.

There were just so many complicating factors. The primary one being a time difference. A time difference of one hundred eighty years.

He put his palms on his forehead.

"I have to go," she said, "before we both get into trouble." She walked past him, her full skirt brushing up against him.

"My intentions are honorable," he said.

She stopped and turned. Tilted her head to look up at him. They still wore their masks, but he barely even noticed it now.

Her lips turned into a smile. "Good," she said and, turning, swept from the room.

And left him standing there.

His heart in his throat.

At least now he knew what to do.

CHAPTER 5

*C*amille pulled the hood of her cloak over her head and slipped out the back door. With her mother at the plantation and her father still abed after a late night gambling, it was surprisingly easy to move about unnoticed.

Though the sun had peaked over the horizon, it was difficult to see through the early morning mist drifting off the river. She knew her way well enough, though, to be unhindered.

She slipped down the street, turned left, and hurried toward the river. As the Saint Louis Cathedral tolled the morning call to prayer from the belltower, she sent up a silent prayer. *Please forgive me Father for I am about to sin.*

Turning down an alleyway, she ignored the shadows moving about in the fog and shored up her courage. She needed information and Madam Laveau was the only one who could give it.

The answers she sought could not be found in the Cathedral or even in her father's library.

Only in the questionable world of shadows. She stood at Madam Laveau's green door, locked in indecision. She'd been here once before – but it had been years ago – with her brothers. Richard and Samuel had been born less than a year apart. Thick as thieves, they could have been twins. Camille came along one year later – always the younger sister. Her mother liked to say that she got her childbearing over with quickly.

She could ride a horse as well as either of them and could shoot a gun as well, too. But Camille excelled at math. And once she learned something, she never forgot. She'd been eleven when they had visited Madam Laveau. They wanted to know their fortunes. The fortune-teller had sent them away. She told them to never come back and to forget that she even existed. They must have done so, because they had never spoken of returning.

Camille, however, never forgot.

She knocked on the door and held her breath.

And waited for what seemed like an interminable amount of time. Perhaps she had come too early. Nonetheless, legend said that she only took visitors either at dawn or Midnight by appointment.

Finally, the door opened and a woman of indiscernible age opened the door and looked her up and down. The woman, also wearing a hood, was dressed in black lace, head to toe.

Camille exhaled slowly. Despite her reputation, Madam Laveau had an air of kindness.

"Camille Lafluer," she said. "I've been expecting you."

Camille gasped and took a step back.

"No need to fear, she continued, "come inside." She stepped back and held the door wide for Camille to follow.

Camille stepped through the doorway. The little room had curtains hanging all around all the walls. A small sofa bumped up against one side of the little room. A table stood on the other side. The table was covered with candles of various sizes, their flames casting shadows across the room.

"Sit," Madame Laveau said.

Camille sat on the sofa and the older woman sat next to her.

"You're here about your young man," Madam Laveau stated.

Camille was stunned. She glanced around the room.

"I don't need a crystal ball to see what's going on."

"You can read my mind," Camille said. This was much, too much, unnerving.

Madame Laveau smiled to herself. "I'm sorry. I'm frightening you." She reaching out, placed a hand over Camille's. "Tell me why you're here."

Camille felt a little jolt shoot between them. Or perhaps she imagined it. "I'm really not sure. Perhaps I shouldn't have come."

"Nonsense. You're looking for answers and you hoped I could help you."

Camille nodded.

"Tell me about him," Madame Laveau said.

Camille inhaled deeply. Steadied herself. She was here. She may as well jump right in. "He told me he's from the future."

"I see." The older woman did not appear to be surprised. "What else did he tell you?"

"Nothing. I haven't spoken to him since."

"You don't know whether or not to believe him."

"I just need to know if it's possible."

Madame Laveau squeezed her hand. "Anything is possible. All you have to do is believe."

Camille shook her head. "Not true. I used to believe in unicorns, but they're merely a mythical creature. They don't exist."

"You're strong-willed, you are.

Camille lifted her chin and stared into the older woman's eyes. "I believe in facts and logic," she said.

"Then this will be difficult for you. But you'll get along well with your man from the future."

"Why do you say that?"

"They, too, put very little stock in things that don't make sense to them."

Camille tore her gaze away, unable to tolerate the unblinking stare any longer.

"You must have an open mind," the woman continued.

"I know what I saw," Camille blurted.

"Good." Madame Laveau studied Camille. Camille held herself still, her gaze straight ahead, refusing to squirm under her perusal. "You've seen more than most."

Camille turned back to her. "Tell me what you know."

"There's a woman in Natchez. A woman who was spelled by an ancient Druid. The woman is able to move freely about through time. The spell, some say, passed to her grandchildren."

"Then it's possible."

"Oh, ma chère, it's more than possible."

"How do you know?"

"I have faith."

"You've seen it?"

"It's not something you can see."

"But I saw it. I saw him disappear."

"Then you, my child, should have no questions."

"I thought he might be a ghost."

Madame Laveau waved her hand in dismissal. "You're not dealing with ghosts here."

"How do you know?"

"What color are his eyes?"

"Blue."

"There," Madam Laveau said. "He's not a ghost. Ghosts are transparent. They don't have eye color. I've seen my fair share of them and I've even had conversations with a few. But never have I a seen a ghost with eye color. No, ma chère, you spoke with a living, breathing man."

"But…"

"A living breathing man from the future."

After Camille put a handful of coins in the woman's hand, she hastened outside and sucked fresh air into her lungs.

So it was true. Or at least possible. Bradley may very well be from the future.

BRADLEY MONITORED THE GAUGES ON HIS CONSOLE AS THE wheels of the little Cessna airplane touched down on the Natchez-Adams County Airport runway. His grandfather stood leaning against his white Lexus sedan. Bradley smiled. His grandfather was nothing, if not reliable.

At a bigger airport, there would have been a car available for a quick dash into town, but not here. Besides, his grandfather delighted in picking him up.

He taxied over and turned off the engine a few yards from his grandfather's car.

He gathered up his briefcase and climbed out of the plane.

"It's good to see you," His grandfather, Jonathan, said, pulling him into a hug.

"You too. I'm sorry it's been so long."

They drove into town and parked in front of the Biscuits and Blues restaurant on Main Street. After taking a seat by the window, they ordered shrimp poboys.

"Something must be on your mind," Jonathan said, "to fly all the way up here."

"It's just a hop, skip, and a jump," Bradley said, but a pang of guilt shot through him. It had been at last six months since he'd seen his grandfather.

After he'd gotten out of the hospital, Bradley had stayed with him for two weeks, taking only a couple of short flights for local customers. He and Jonathan had always been close, but they had bonded during that time while Jonathan recuperated.

"Maybe on that little Cessna. A bit longer in a car."

Bradley nodded. "How have you been?"

"I've been good. Still missing the girls."

The girls were Vaughn, Bradley's grandmother who had died nearly two years ago and Erika, Bradley's sister who had been gone for nearly a year.

"Yeah," Bradley said. Bradley gazed around. Took a deep breath and exhaled slowly.

"You might as well spit it out," Jonathan said.

Bradley heaved a sigh. His grandfather was right. If he was going to do this, he needed to get it over with. "You know how we talked and decided that there must something about the house that allowed Ericka to... travel?"

Jonathan nodded. Waited.

"It might have been the house for her, but it seems there's more to it."

"You?" Jonathan murmured.

Bradley nodded. "In New Orleans." He took out his phone and showed his grandfather the photo of the hotel, first without the bar, then with the bar.

"You went in," Jonathan said.

Bradley nodded. "The first time was by accident."

"And the next?"

"The next two were... not exactly by accident, but not exactly explainable either."

Jonathan leaned back in his chair, staring into space as he seemed to consider. Then he turned his gaze back to his grandson. "There's more to it," he said.

Bradley swiped to the next image on his phone to the picture of Camille – the one he had zoomed and cropped. Even though he had memorized every curve of her face, his pulse quickened at the sight of her image on his phone as he turned it for Jonathan to see.

Jonathan took his phone, studied the picture. Reaching

over, Bradley swiped to the next picture. The original one showing Camille from a distance in the smoky bar – with other men in the photo.

Jonathan's eyes widened as he stared at the image.

"Watch this," Bradley said, holding his finger on the image, allowing the image to go live for three seconds.

Despite the shock on his grandfather's face, it felt good to share with someone else. Someone else who had an inkling of what he was looking at.

"Bradley," Jonathan said, then waiting as the server set their food on the table. After the server walked away, he turned his gaze to his grandson. "Is this what I think it is?"

"As far as I can tell."

"My God, Bradley, do you know what you have here?"

"I know." Bradley took his phone, closed it. And took a bite of his sandwich.

Ignoring his food, Jonathan held out his hand. "Can I see her picture again?"

"Of course," Bradley said, pulling the picture of Camille back up.

"She's pretty," Jonathan said. "What's her name?"

"Camille Lafleur."

"I knew some Lafleurs. What year is it?"

"1838."

Jonathan nodded, handed the phone back, and bit into his sandwich. "You'll go back," he said, his voice resigned.

"I don't know if I can," Bradley said.

"But the important thing is whether you will if you can."

His grandfather was right. That was an important distinction.

"And," Jonathan continued, pushing his plate aside. "Whether or not you plan to stay." Jonathan put a hand beneath his glasses, wiping at his eyes. "You've got to decide if Camille is the one you want to be with. And if so, is she worth giving up your life as you know it."

Jonathan opened his eyes and glued his gaze to Bradley's. Bradley swallowed the lump in his throat. He had a feeling Jonathan wasn't talking just about him anymore. He wasn't sure what to say. The indecision must have been reflected in his face.

"The first couple of times are probably accidental," Jonathan said. "Or least they seem to be. But then you get to make a choice. You get to decide whether or not to go back to the place where it happens. Then all bets are off. Then the door closes when you least expect it and you're locked into the past."

Bradley stared at his grandfather. "How do you know this? Erika?"

Jonathan nodded. "Erika, yes, but even before that, Vaughn."

His grandfather's words sent shock waves through his system. His grandmother – who had died in a boating accident… "What do you mean Vaughn?"

"You know what," Jonathan said signaling for the check. "Let's go by the house. Do you have time? I want to give you something anyway."

"Sure." Bradley glanced at his phone. "I have time." He'd cleared his calendar until he could figure out what he was going to do next. His grandfather was right. The next decision was up to him.

Did he stay away and go on with his life as he knew it? Or did he risk giving it all up by seeking out the girl who tugged at his heart?

Jonathan drove to the plantation house where Bradley had spent his summers and many holidays. Bradley knew that his mother drove down at least a couple of times a month to check on Jonathan and help out with things around the house.

Since it was a pretty day outside, Bradley grabbed a soda

from the refrigerator and sat on the back porch while Jonathan went upstairs to retrieve something.

He sat in a chair and watched as two squirrels chased each other down a tree limb. His mother had planted spring flowers all over the backyard, so there was a splash of color spilling from the porch into the backyard.

Jonathan sat in the chair next to him. "Want a cigar?" he asked.

Bradley shook his head. Jonathan lit a cigar and inhaled deeply. "Nothing better," he said.

"You're getting used to living here alone?" Bradley asked.

"Sure," Jonathan said. "You live and adapt."

They sat in silence for a few minutes. Bradley shifted in his chair. Waited.

"It's time someone besides me knows what happened," Jonathan said. "I'm tired of carrying it all by myself."

"What is it Grandpa?"

"Vaughn. Vaughn wasn't from this time."

Bradley felt his heart rate quicken. "What do you mean?"

Jonathan blew out his breath and gazed toward the window as though looking into his memory. "I don't know everything, mind you. But Vaughn was born in France."

Bradley nodded. He knew that about his grandmother. Jonathan, however, no longer saw him. He was deep in his memories.

"She was born in the 1700s. She had just gotten to America when she was attacked by Indians. Somehow someone saved her life and she ended up in the 1800s."

"But she lived here."

"She was here for a time."

Bradley hesitated, then blurted out the question that he had to know. "Did she really die?"

"I'm not sure," Jonathan said. "She was very mysterious about it. But she made it clear that she wouldn't be back.

Somehow, I think she thought her ability to... travel was running out."

"Vaughn was a time traveler."

Jonathan looked back at him then. Focused. "Yes. Your grandmother was a time-traveler."

"She could still be alive."

He shook his head. "Not to me. I'll never see her again."

A little kindling of hope shot through Bradley. "But she could be alive," he insisted.

Jonathan didn't answer. Instead, he reached into his pocket, and pulled out his silver pocket watch. "I want to give you this," he said. "Vaughn had it made for me. In the 1800s." He held it out to Bradley.

Bradley took the pocket watch from his grandfather. He'd seen it before, but he was only now learning of its significance.

The watch was just under about three inches around and had an open face.

"It was made in Paris by LeRoy," Jonathan said, pride evident in his voice.

"How did she have it made?" Bradley asked.

Jonathan shook his head. "Your grandmother was a resourceful woman. I don't know how she did the things she did."

"I can't take this from you," Bradley said.

"You aren't taking it. I'm giving it to you. You're the only person left who can appreciate it. Anyone else would just see it as junk to be thrown out. But that watch was made for me...in 1837."

Bradley smiled at his grandfather. "That's..." he stopped in mid-thought, his throat suddenly thick with emotion.

"Take it," Jonathan said. "Perhaps you can pass it along to your own son."

"I will," Bradley said, turning away so his grandfather couldn't see the tears welling in his eyes. If he did this thing – if he went back in time – and stayed, his grandfather would never meet any children he might have.

"Come with me," Bradley blurted.

"Oh no. Don't think I haven't thought about it. Even with Vaughn, we tried to figure out a way, but it doesn't seem to work that way. Besides, I'm old. I need medical care."

Bradley considered his grandfather. Other than a brief illness due to poisoning, Jonathan had always been in good health. "Is there something you haven't told me?" he asked.

Jonathan waved him off. "I'm healthy as a horse. Right now. But I'm not getting any younger."

Bradley sipped his soda and gazed through the window into the sitting area – the television, the electric lights. The air conditioning. It was selfish, he decided, to ask someone else to give up their life for him. He was thankful his sister hadn't asked him to go back in time with her. It wasn't a decision he would have wanted to make. Besides, like his grandfather said, it didn't work like that. Whatever it was that gave him the ability to go back in time appeared to be tailored only toward him. "You're right," he conceded.

Jonathan nodded. "Like I said, it doesn't work like that."

"It may not work for me again, anyway."

"There's only one way to find out," Jonathan said.

CHAPTER 6

*B*radley pressed his palms against the rail that overlooked the Mississippi River. This was day four of what he'd come to think of as his New Orleans trek. For one who didn't like the Crescent City, he was spending an awful lot of time here lately.

He'd come back a week after meeting with his grandfather. The first night he had walked around and around like a mad wolf until midnight, then gone up to his room and collapsed in exhaustion.

The second night he had loitered around the front of the hotel, pacing back and forth.

The third night he had decided the spell or whatever it was had worn off and he wasn't going back in time again. He resigned himself to thinking it was somehow connected to Mardi Gras. So he would have to wait until next year before trying again. Nonetheless, he'd walked around for awhile trying to recreate the circumstances that had been in place when it had happened before.

In the meantime, he'd cashed in a significant amount of his savings on 1830s currency and coins. Even now, the coins felt heavy in his jacket pocket. He'd wiped out three different collectors. Though he'd gotten some odd looks, none of them had questioned him too much. Apparently coin and currency collectors were an obsessive group of individuals, accustomed to quirkiness.

Glancing over his shoulder, he noted that the storm was moving in a little quicker than forecasted. A raindrop splashed on the back of his hand. Much quicker than forecasted. As he hurried down the boardwalk, the sky opened up and Bradley was drenched within minutes.

He got to the street and took off running. He wasn't worried so much about getting wet, himself, but he wanted to protect the paper money in his pocket.

As was habit, he glanced toward the brick wall before entering the hotel. No door.

He hurried up to his room and after quickly drying off with a towel, took the paper money from his pocket.

He groaned. The precious bills were soaked, their ink smeared and staining his clothes. He took the money and, dabbing each one with a dry cloth, spread the money out on the dresser. It would have to dry before he would know if it would be salvageable. He dried the coins and tucked them into his suitcase.

He shrugged out of the rest of his clothes and jumped into the hot shower. He heard thunder from the storm even over the running water. It was decision time. He couldn't keep just hanging around here. Only a madman would do that. He was teetering on the edge of sanity as it were.

It was time to pull the plug on this whole endeavor. Perhaps he would come back next year at Mardi Gras and try again.

The hot water helped him clear his head. It was time to get back to work and to his life.

After toweling off, he pulled on a pair of jeans and a T-shirt. As had become his new habit, he put his grandfather's pocket watch in his pocket. He never checked it. He just carried it around. The habit of checking his phone or his iPad for the time was too entrenched.

His mind made up, he pulled out his iPad and scheduled a flight out of here for the morning. And scheduled a flight for a client for the next day.

As he took care of reclaiming his life, the storm raged overhead. The electricity blinked twice and went off. He waited for the generator, but apparently, the old hotel didn't have one.

He walked down three flights of stairs and joined the crowd in the lobby. The manager had brought out several bottles of wine and was in the process of pouring wine for the disgruntled guests.

Bradley took a glass of red wine from the manager he recognized from his first day here. The day he had so desperately searched for the Le Bon Temps Roule

"Hey," the man said. "Did you um… find what you were looking for."

Bradley shook his head. "Turns out you were right. One glass too many and I got all turned around."

The manager nodded. "Happens all the time. No worries."

Bradley took his glass of wine and wandered to the front door of the hotel. The rain fell in torrents and lightening grazed the building.

Someone had left a red umbrella by the door. Bradley picked it and glanced behind at the crowd in the lobby. No one seemed to be paying any attention to the storm, must less to him.

He opened the door, popped open the umbrella, and stepped out into the storm. A gust of wind whipped at the umbrella, threatening to tear it from his hands, and subsequently leaving him little protection from the rain.

Like metal to a magnet, he was drawn to the right, toward the doorway that wasn't. With the rain, and the wind, and the umbrella whipping about, he could barely see, but he knew approximately the distance to the door to the Le Bon Temps Roule.

As a crash of thunder shook the air, he opened the door, and all but fell inside to the quietness of the bar.

Unlike his previous entrances, this time all eyes were on him. He heard their murmurs.

"Didn't know it was raining outside."

"Must be mad to be out in this."

"Is he wearing his undergarments?"

Bradley closed his umbrella and stood it on the floor next to him. Standing there, drenched, wearing his jeans and a T-shirt, the only coherent thought in his head was *I didn't bring the money.*

How many hours had he spent acquiring authentic 1830s money? Making sure he was dressed appropriately?

And here he stood, in nothing more than jeans and white T-shirt without a dime to his name. With a bubble of panic, he realized he'd even left his cell phone in the hotel room.

I can't use it here anyway.

He swallowed a laugh of what could only be desperation.

After all his preparation, he stood here with nothing more than a stolen red umbrella and a glass of wine to his name.

It had been a week. Not that she was counting, mind you, but a week nonetheless. After the odd conversation with Bradley about her betrothal status and his honorable intentions, he had slipped away without her seeing him again. Whether by design or accident, she didn't know.

She only knew that she had watched for him over the next few days. The day after Mardis Gras ended, her father had not allowed her to work in the tavern. She'd moped around that evening and all of the next day until he had begrudgingly permitted her to work two hours at sunset. He refused to allow her to work after darkness settled over the city. "It's just not fitting," he'd said.

Nonetheless, she found that if she sat quietly in a corner and read her book, he didn't say anything.

Although they didn't speak of it, she was certain he knew she waited for him. The handsome man who may very well be from the future. Of course, she didn't dare tell him that. Nor did she tell him about her little visit with Madame Laveau. He would have locked her in her room for sure. Or worse, he would have banished her to the plantation to spend the summer with her mother.

So, she kept her head down and avoided her father's attention as much as possible.

She had worked her two hours, glad to be free of the mask worn during the Mardi Gras period, and settled at the back of the tavern. Her father wasn't home tonight. He'd told her he had business across town. He didn't elaborate and she didn't ask. Sometimes she wondered if her father kept a mistress. It wasn't uncommon in their wealthy circle. That was certainly something she could never ask her father.

Staring at the letters on the page, more than actually reading, her attention was drawn to a commotion at the front of the tavern, near the door.

She stood up, the book falling from her hands. Through the haziness from the cigar smoke, she saw him. Standing there, dripping wet, one hand resting on the handle of a red umbrella and the other holding a glass of wine. But it was his clothing that stood out. He wore britches and an…. Undershirt?

She moved toward him, and now she could see his expression. His eyes wide, he stared into space. Grabbing up her skirts in two fists, she dashed toward him – a protective instinct involuntarily taking over any coherent thoughts.

Reaching him, she took him by the arm and led him toward

the back of the tavern toward their private area. He went compliantly. Neither of them speaking.

They reached the back office and she pulled a chair out for him, and nudged him into it. After taking the wine and umbrella from his hands, she knelt next to him and gazed into his face. He blinked and smiled. "Are you real?" He asked.

She nodded, feeling the corners of her lips lifting. "Are you?"

"You have to forgive me," he said.

Her frown returned. "Forgive you? For what?"

"I didn't bring the money."

He must be daft. "Money?" Perhaps he was still concerned with the membership fee. "You already paid your fee. There's no need for money."

He scoffed. "That's a good thing," he said.

Camille had never seen a man, other than her brothers in an undershirt. He had no sign of blood. Nonetheless… "Are you wounded?" She asked.

He was staring at her now. Smiling again. He inhaled deeply. "No."

She got up and dragged a chair next to him. Sitting, she faced him. "You came back."

His grin widened. "I did."

"I didn't think you would."

He kept his eyes on hers. "You have no idea how difficult it was."

"I'm sorry," she said. "But I'm glad you're here."

"Me too."

Marcus came to the door. "Miss?" He asked. "Is everything well?"

"Everything is good, Marcus. Thank you," Camille said, without breaking her gaze with Bradley.

Marcus turned away.

"Wait," Camille said. "Marcus, bring me a towel and one of Father's shirts."

"You aren't wearing your mask," Bradley said after Marcus had left them.

"You aren't wearing your... clothes."

Perplexed, Bradley glanced down. "This is a casual outfit."

"From the future," she added.

He nodded.

"It's all right," she said. "I believe you."

"How could you possibly?"

"I can't really tell you. But I consulted."

"Hmm."

"No need to worry," she said. "No one knows."

"I hope you're right. I'd be burned at the stake."

"Oh no. That doesn't happen anymore."

Marcus returned and handed Bradley a towel, then a shirt. He held it out at arm's length and watched Bradley warily. After Marcus had left again, Bradley said, "he knows."

"Who? Marcus?"

Bradley dried off, then shrugged into the shirt and began buttoning the buttons. "He suspects something."

"Marcus suspects everyone. It's his job. He's supposed to look out for me."

"It's a good thing I'm not dangerous then."

She studied him. "You? You don't look like the dangerous sort to me." In fact, he looked rather vulnerable. Her father's shirt was little too small in the shoulders for Bradley.

THINGS HAD NOT GONE AS PLANNED. BRADLEY HAD PLANNED everything. He had enough money to present himself as a man of some means and he had procured appropriate clothing.

Instead he had given up on ever returning to 1838 and had stumbled back in time when he least expected it. When he had been most unprepared. In fact, he felt less prepared, somehow, than the first time he had time-traveled.

It was silly, but he felt a sense of panic at not having his cell phone with him. *I'm a product of my time.* Logically, he knew he couldn't use it even if he had it with him, but he was having a visceral reaction to the knowledge that he had left it behind.

"I can't stay," he blurted.

"All right," she said, appearing unaffected by his statement.

"I have to go, but I'll be right back," he said. *I'll be indigent. A man can't survive without money.*

She smiled. "I understand."

"I left something upstairs in the hotel room."

"I'll wait here," she said.

Bradley stood up, but wasn't sure which way to go. "Is there a back door?" He asked.

"Of course." She, too, stood up and led him down a hallway to a wooden door with a lock on it. She took a large ring of keys from her skirt pocket and opened the lock. "Just walk around that corner and you'll be on the street," she told him, gesturing to the left.

"Thank you," Bradley said, squeezing her hand before dashing toward the street. He just needed to go upstairs and get his things.

But when he reached the street, he was nearly run over by a horse and rider. The street was dirt, dusty despite the recent rain storm. He ran a hand down his still damp jeans.

This isn't right.

It's the wrong door.

He turned and retraced his steps. Camille still stood at the door watching him.

"I have to go out the front," he said.

She raised an eyebrow.

"I'm sorry," he said. "I know I'm not dressed properly."

"Wait," she said, and disappeared down the hallway. Within

minutes, she returned with a jacket. "This is my father's. You can borrow it."

"Thank you," he said and slipped into the wool jacket. "I'll come right back."

"All right," she said, a strange smile on her lips.

Although he preferred not to face the room full of men again, he entered the smoky tavern and kept his eyes focused on the door. If they spoke about him or even to him, he kept it tuned out as he hastened toward the door. The door to the street that would put him back in his world.

He reached the door and shoved it open. It occurred to him in that moment that he had forgotten his umbrella.

But as he stepped through the threshold, he stepped once again, onto the dusty, dirt street. With horses tied to the posts and men in top hats rushing to and fro.

Determined, he turned left and went down the street toward the hotel.

He walked through the lobby and stopped where the elevator should be. Instead he faced a wall.

Slowly, he turned and walked back to the hotel lobby. The room was lit with candles. Everything was different. More... plush. Blue velvet curtains and settees. The walls were painted maroon with scrolls of flowers painted here and there. A man and woman sat, their heads bent together over a paper. The man was dressed in a dark gray suit and the woman wore a long gown with an elaborate headpiece.

It was quiet. No cars. No elevators. No electric anything.

Just quiet.

He dropped onto an empty sofa and stared at nothing. His mind frozen.

He'd done it. He'd gone back in time.

Again.

Only this time he hadn't returned home after he walked out through the door front.

He put his head in his hands and tried to think.

Instead, his mind raced with no coherent thoughts.

He felt someone sit down next to him.

"Are you all right?" Camille asked.

He lifted his head and looked into her lovely green eyes. The green eyes that had haunted his every waking minute since he'd first seen her. Eyes that infiltrated his dreams and, like a siren's song, pulled him toward her.

She had on white gloves now and a shawl over her shoulders. She placed a gloved hand on his shoulder. "What can I do?" She asked.

"I just wanted to run upstairs and get my things."

"Upstairs." She lowered her voice to a whisper. "In the future?"

He nodded. "Yes. It would only take a minute."

"I don't think it's all that easy. Madame Laveau says it doesn't work like that."

"Who?"

"Just a wise woman who lives in town."

"The one with a black cat and a three-legged dog?"

She gazed at him as though he'd possibly gone insane.

"Nevermind." He shook his head. "Well, did she happen to say how it does work?"

"She said it's complicated."

"What am I supposed to do?" He asked, searching those green eyes, looking for answers. It had all seemed so simple. Just get here and all would be well.

"I don't know," she said.

He took a deep steadying breath. There had to be a solution. Perhaps he just needed to go back into the tavern and try again.

"I think you're going to be here awhile," she said.

"Why do you say that?"

"Madame Laveau."

"Right." He nodded. The one who apparently knew more

about this time-travel thing than he did. Right now anyone would do as well at figuring it out. He stood up. Paced. Ran a hand through his hair. He knew he was drawing attention to himself. Pacing about in his wet blue jeans.

"There's nothing to be done about it tonight," she said, her voice laced with calmness.

"Come back to the tavern. We have a guest room you can stay in. We'll figure it out tomorrow."

She was right, of course. He should have had a contingency plan. He laughed out loud. A contingency plan for traveling back in time. As though having a plan at all weren't ridiculous enough.

No. He needed to think. To sleep. To regroup.

As he followed her from the hotel, made the familiar walk to the tavern door, it occurred to him that he had gotten exactly what he'd wanted.

CHAPTER 7

*C*amille led Bradley around to the back door of their townhouse. She wasn't about to parade him through the crowded tavern again. Especially not in his current state. He looked... unwell.

He quietly followed her upstairs to the sleeping quarters. She grabbed a candle from a wall sconce and led him into the blue guestroom on the west side. It was the only true guest room in the townhouse. She refused to count her brothers' rooms as guestrooms. They would be back. That's what she told herself to combat the butterflies in her stomach when she worried about them fighting Indians in Texas. Keeping their room ready kept some of the anxiety at bay. That, and the silent prayers she sent up each time she passed by their rooms.

Going into the darkened room, she lit a candle on the nightstand, then went to open the thick velvet curtains to allow moonlight to infuse the room.

He stood just inside the doorway, watching her, seemingly at a loss. Her heart went out to this man. This man who had found himself in a foreign time. She could not even begin to fathom what his time must be like. She could only liken it to a foreign country – with different dress and different customs.

Nonetheless, some divine intervention had landed him here in her time. Divine intervention, otherwise, how would two people with such undeniable attraction have found each other – across time itself.

He hadn't caught up with her line of thinking. That much was obvious to her. Madame Laveau had cautioned her that in the future, people were much less likely to put stock in things that couldn't be explained.

And this definitely could not be explained.

She went to him and, taking his hand, led him to the settee in front of the window. The moon was visible from here. It shone brightly tonight. It almost looked like she could reach out and touch it. "The moon is pretty tonight," she commented as she sat next to him.

He glanced out the window and nodded absently.

"You have the same moon?" she asked.

He turned his gaze to her then, blinked, and seemed to notice her for the first time since they had sat in the hotel lobby. His lips curved into a smile. He chuckled. "Yes, we have the same moon. It looks no worse for wear."

"That's a relief," she said, smiling brightly. At least she had managed to shake him from his daze. "What year is it in your time?"

"2017."

She breathed in deeply to steady herself. How different the world must be from now. She did some quick math in her head and tried to imagine what it would be like in 1658. Simpler times. She couldn't even begin to wrap her head around it. Perhaps she would go to the library so that she could have some perspective. He must think them simple.

"What is it like?" She asked.

"Everything is different," he said.

"Everything?"

He shook his head. "If I had my phone… my things… I could show you. Everything started to change so quickly that in a hundred years, the world is no longer anything like it was before."

"It sounds a little frightening," she said.

"It actually is." His gaze was intent on hers now. She almost regretted pulling him out of his daze. It occurred to her that she shouldn't be alone with him here in this bedroom. Her father was out and no one else was home. There were servants about and the way they had a propensity to gossip, she mustn't be caught here alone with him.

"I have to go now," she said. "You should get some sleep and I'll do the same. In the morning, we'll try to figure out what to do about… your… situation."

He nodded. Released a deep breath. "That's the best we have then," he said. "Good night, Camille."

She left him, went down the hallway to her room, closed the thick wooden door and locked it. She leaned against it and closed her eyes. Her wish had come true.

Yet she felt compelled to lock the door behind her.

She wasn't sure if she locked him out or locked herself in.

BRADLEY WATCHED CAMILLE LEAVE HIM. TAMPED DOWN THE urge to call her back. She was the only thing familiar to him. The only thing that he trusted to keep him safe in this foreign time.

He stared at the moon. He hadn't told her, but it looked bigger. Brighter. Had the earth's rotation changed? He didn't remember ever reading about that. It was something he would look up when… if he ever got back to his time.

There were so many things he wanted to look up.

But the thing he was most interested in had just breezed out of his room and disappeared down the hall. He had worked so very hard to get back to her. Planned. Shopped. He had wanted everything to be perfect.

Now here he was with nothing to his name but an umbrella and a glass of wine – both of which he had left downstairs, probably never to see again.

And he wore blue jeans and T-shirt. And, of course, a borrowed jacket, but that didn't count.

But the thing that bothered him most was his lack of funds. How was he supposed to survive without money? Or worse, skills?

What could an airplane pilot possibly do for income in 1838?

Surely there would be some type of job, he assured himself.

Camille was right. He needed to sleep. He got up, wandered around the room. Much as he had been in the hotel lobby, he was struck by the plushness of the furnishings. He studied the tall bureau, so tall, he couldn't even see over the top of it, and opened the doors. There was nothing inside. Camille had mentioned something about this being a guest room, though he'd hardly heard a word she had said.

It was as though his ears had been ringing. Bradley hadn't been in the military, but his best friend from high school had been. His friend had described the blast from an IED that hit several yards away as being so severe, that he'd been left with an intense ringing in his ears and a disorientation.

Travelling through time was like being in the wake of an IED blast then. *It hadn't been like that the other times.*

It was impossible to ignore the little voice that told him this time was different.

He didn't want to think about the implications of what that meant. He slipped out of his wet jeans, spread them over a chair to dry, and after climbing into the bed, buried himself beneath the covers.

As soon as he closed his eyes, his mind went into overdrive.

Tomorrow he would work on getting home. His money he'd left out to dry should still be there. Most of all, he needed the coins. After a crash course in money collecting, he's determined that the coins were much more valuable.

Once he drifted into sleep, the nightmares started. Only this time, the nightmare didn't involve losing control of an aircraft. This nightmare had him walking up and down the muddied streets of New Orleans, hungry, wet, with no place to go. Well dressed men pushed him aside with their canes. Elegantly dressed women turned away from him in disgust, holding their skirts high, walking as far around him as they could get. One of them was Camille, wrinkling her nose at him.

He woke in a sweat. His worst fear was coming true. He was here with no means. No future. No place in this world.

Staring at the ceiling, he came to a decision. He had to get back to his time.

CAMILLE WAS UP BEFORE DAWN. SHE WANTED TO OPEN Bradley's door – just to peek and see if he was still here. But she didn't. Instead, she put her energies into procuring clothing for him. Bradley was about the same size as her brother Samuel. Tamping down the feelings of guilt, she raided his bureau, dragging out every piece of clothing. Bradley had nothing. Fortunately, her brother had kept a nice supply of clothing here at the townhouse. She knew he had more at the plantation and had taken the most useful items with him, but this would keep Bradley from standing out and having attention drawn to him.

He was going to have a hard enough time fitting in without having decent clothes to wear.

Her arms laden with clothes, she went to his door and kicked at it with her foot. It seemed like forever before he opened the door.

His face lit up when he saw her and he grabbed the clothes spilling from her arms.

"What's all this?" he asked.

"My brother, Samuel's, clothes. There's more if you want to help me," she said, waiting while he dumped the clothes on the bed.

"Sure," he said, following her down the hall to her brother's room. "Are you sure he won't mind."

"He has plenty more out at the plantation house," she said. "You'll have to try them on, but I think you're about his size."

"And if he minds?" Bradley persisted as she filled his arms with more clothes, stacking shoes on top.

"If he minds, you can give them back." She said, closing the bureau doors. "You're fortunate that you're tall like Samuel because Samuel likes clothes. My other brother Richard doesn't care as much for clothes. He'll wear any old thing. Fortunately, he's much shorter than you."

She turned, and seeing him, giggled. She had stacked the clothes so high she could no longer see his face.

"I don't think I'm gonna need all this much." His voice was muffled behind the load of clothing.

"We'll bring back what you can't wear or what you don't like." She took his arm and led him toward the door.

"I'm at your mercy," he said.

"Don't worry. I won't lead you down a flight of stairs or anything."

He mumbled something, but she couldn't make it out.

She chewed her lip as she led him back toward the guest room. The worst challenge was yet to come. He may think he was at her mercy, but it was her father's mercy that would truly tell the tale. Her father could easily send him on his way. In fact... "We're here," she said, taking the shoes off the top and working her way down.

Her brain began to work overtime. In order to convince her

father, they needed a better story than *he just happened to land here from another time*. No. Her father was plenty generous. But generosity only went so far. Bradley wasn't exactly a puppy she found on the street. He was living breathing man. A stranger.

There was no one to vouch for him.

And without a proper introduction, her father would not be overly thrilled with his daughter taking up with a stranger.

"I need to get back," he said.

"So you've said."

"Will you help me?"

"How can I help you?"

"I don't know. Let me walk out the front door," he said.

"You can walk out the front door all you want," she decided to leave off the part about it not doing any good. If she were in his shoes, she was fairly certain she, too, would do whatever she could to try to get back to her time.

"Does it bother you?" he asked.

"Does what bother me?"

"Does it bother you that I'm from the future?"

She shrugged and began sorting clothes. Trousers in one pile. Shirts in another. "It doesn't mean that much to me. It's no different than if you'd said you were from Japan."

"It's a little different."

"Not to me. You're still a person. You just have different customs. A different language. Different experiences. But we can still communicate."

What she didn't say was *we can still be attracted to one another*.

"How did you get to be so wise?" he asked. "Did you have to work at it or did it just come natural?"

She laughed. "I'm not wise. That's just the way I see it. I've never been like everyone else."

"How are you different?" he asked, his eyes full of interest now.

She shook her head. "I don't know. I'd rather figure out a

math problem than sew a quilt. I don't like to go to balls just for idle flirting. I'd rather be doing something constructive. Like reading a book or doing some work in the tavern."

He watched her with a goofy expression. "You and I are going to get along just fine," he said.

She felt the heat rise to her cheeks. He tucked a lock of stray hair behind her ear.

"I thought you were about to leave," she said.

He dropped his hand and she immediately regretted her words. But truly, that's all he'd been talking about since his arrival yesterday.

"Just because I have to get home, doesn't mean I won't be coming back," he said.

She stopped sorting and turned to face him. Felt the blood boil in her veins. "How do you know that? How do you know that the number of times you can step through that portal isn't limited? How do you know that you aren't going to have to make a choice at some point? Now... or then?"

He shook his head, once. "I don't," he said softly. "I don't know. You have no idea how hard I worked to get back here. Here. To you. As a man of means. To be worthy of you. Now here I am. With nothing but the shirt on my back. I have nothing to offer you like this. I'm not worthy of giving you the time of day."

Her eyes welled with unshed tears. "I don't care about your wealth. Money can't buy things like health and love. My father has enough money for anything I could ever need. So I know."

"You're right," he said softly. "Money can't buy love. But love can't live without money. I can't call upon you with nothing substantial to offer."

"Then don't call upon me."

He lifted an eyebrow. "Without you, I have no reason to be in 1838."

She swirled and sat on the settee, overcome with dizziness

at his bold statement. Yet she knew he spoke the truth. The first time he had stumbled upon her by chance... or fate. After that, he had purposely sought her out. Risked giving up his way of life to see her again.

"The first thing we have do is to convince my father to let you stay," she said.

He groaned and sat next to her. "How do we do that?"

"I'm not sure yet." She stared into the distance, her mind racing. What could she say that would convince her father to allow Bradley to court her without a proper introduction. Suddenly she brightened. "We can tell him I met you while I was at the boarding school in Natchitoches."

"You went to boarding school? For wayward girls?"

"Wayward? Of course not. It was a finishing school. To make sure we were well versed in dancing, art, poetry, and such."

"You can do all those things?"

"Of course. All young ladies are required to learn such things. Is that no longer the case?"

He shook his head. "Not at all. Those are considered lost arts."

"Oh," she said. "That's unfortunate."

They sat in silence for a few minutes. Then she picked up the thread of their previous conversation. "So we'll tell my father that we met and... became good friends. You followed me here. And though you come from a good family, your father fell upon misfortune and you came here to." She stood up, paced, deep in thought. "You came here to find me, but also to start over without your father's name pulling you down."

She stopped in front of him and looked into his eyes. "You came to start your own business."

· · ·

BRADLEY WATCHED CAMILLE PACE, UNABLE TO TAKE HIS EYES OFF her. He was entranced. Her face was flushed from the excitement of concocting a story that would allow him to be here with her father's approval.

"What business?" he asked, when she stood in front of him, her eyes searching his.

"I don't know. What skill do you have?"

He coughed. *I fly airplanes.* "I don't think I have a skill that would be viable."

"Surely you did you something in the future that you could use here."

He knew he had a goofy grin on his face. But he couldn't help it. No. It was too soon to tell her about the airplanes. Perhaps they had to discuss cars first. He shook his head.

"How did you spend your time?"

Before he was a pilot, he studied a lot. "I studied."

"You were a scholar?" Her face brightened.

"Yes," he agreed. He had definitely spent enough time sitting in the classroom to qualify as a scholar. "I was a scholar," he repeated.

"That's perfect."

"Being a scholar isn't exactly a skill."

"Hmm. No, but means you can read and write. So we can work with that."

He stared at her. His mouth must have fallen open.

"You can read and write, can't you?"

He laughed. A chuckle at first, then all out laughter. He laughed so hard, his eyes teared up.

She scowled at him. She went to the little writing desk in the corner and pulled out a sheet of paper and a feather.

A feather?

"Come here," she said. "Come write something."

He wiped his eyes and went to stand next to her. When she

handed him the feather, he looked at it. "What do I do with this?"

She groaned and took it from him. "You can't write."

"I can too," he said, reaching for the feather. "Give me some ink."

She pulled a cork from a little ink well that sat on the table and handed it to him. He pulled out the chair and sat down. This was going to take some concentration. He dipped the quill into the ink and after pulling it out, began writing his name on the paper. He made a mess. There were pools of ink all over the paper.

"Here. See," he said shifting back so she could see what he had written.

"Anyone can write their own name," she said.

"Really? OK." He turned back. Began scribbling again. Had to dip the feather back into the ink. He wrote. *I am from 2017.*

He held the paper up for her to see.

"I'm impressed," she said. "Good. You can write. That's a relief."

"I don't know anyone who can't write," he said, putting the paper down and laying the feather on top of it.

She grabbed up the paper and tore what he had written into little shreds, then tossed it into the cold fireplace.

He turned and leaned back in the chair to study her. "But how does this help us?"

She put a hand over her mouth and a bubble of laughter escaped.

"What's funny?" he asked.

"You have ink everywhere."

"Great," he said and looked at his hands. He did have ink all over his hands. "Where do I wash?"

"You'll have to use the water in the pitcher, but it won't come off.

"What do you mean it won't come off?" he asked, following her to the pitcher and basin on a little stand in the corner.

"It'll have to fade off." She picked up the basin of water and gestured for him to put his hands over the basin.

He scrubbed, but it only spread the ink. She handed him a cloth, but it only spread the ink to the cloth. And left him with fingers stained with ink.

"This is good," she said. "It makes you look like a scholar."

He shook his head. "It makes me look like an idiot."

"No," she said, serious now. She took the cloth and rubbed some ink from his cheek.

"Are you putting ink on my face?" he asked.

"I'm trying to get the ink off of you."

Nonetheless, his skin burned beneath her touch.

"It's barely noticeable now," she said.

"I have to at least try to get back to my time and get the money."

"You with your money. Go ahead then. Each time your chances of getting back lessen."

"Maybe."

"Maybe? Did you notice how long it took you this last time?"

He had noticed. "I want to visit Madame Laveau," he said.

Her eyes widened. "I don't know if that's a good idea."

"Perhaps she can help me figure this thing out."

"Men have disappeared while visiting with her."

"But surely it would be safe if you take me."

"I suppose. Let me think about it. We can only visit her at Midnight."

Of course. Legends had to start somewhere. And meeting a voodoo priestess at Midnight was as good a place to start as any. "Very well," he said. "I should put on something more appropriate."

"Yes!" she said, her face brightening. "Let's pick out

something for you to wear." She quickly moved to the bed and within minutes had picked out some black slacks – or trousers as she called them, a white shirt, and a black jacket.

"Is this casual wear?" he asked.

"It's for everyday, yes."

He stood holding the clothes she'd handed him.

"Oh," she said, "I'll just go down the hall to my room for a few minutes."

After she had closed the door behind her, Bradley sat on the settee, the strange clothes clutched to his chest, and heaved a sigh.

What do I do now?

With her there, distracting him with her deep green eyes and enigmatic smile, he couldn't think. He needed to think. To figure out the best course of action. He studied his hands, stained with ink.

A scholar. What kind of trade was that?

It seems being literate wasn't a given in 1838. Nonetheless, what kind of occupation went with being a scholar?

If only there was something he could do with his knowledge of aviation.

If his memory served, hot air balloons were coming into existence about this time, but Bradley had never had any interest in that. Too many uncontrollable factors.

First things first.

He pulled himself up mentally and got into the clothes Camille had loaned him. She was right. They fit perfectly. He would have preferred a little less ruffle on his shirt and he had certainly never worn heels before, except maybe on a pair of cowboy boots he'd bought on a whim and only worn once.

He had only begun to fold up the mounds of clothes when someone knocked on the door. Expecting to see Camille, he went over and threw open the door. Instead, a tall, black man he remembered seeing downstairs stood at the door. "Mistress

Camille asked me to invite you to the dining room for breakfast."

"Thank you," he said, wondering if he was supposed to go now with Marcus or if it was just a general invitation.

Marcus remained at the door. "Would you like me to lead the way?"

"Please," Bradley said, closing the door behind him and following Marcus down the hall and down a flight of stairs.

Despite the dining room Marcus spoke of being empty, the sidebar was loaded with fresh fruit, eggs, bacon, and a variety of other breakfast foods.

"Help yourself," Marcus said. "If you need anything, just tug on that cord hanging there next to the door."

Bradley filled his plate and sat alone at the dining table. Camille had deserted him, he mused. Not so surprising. She doubtlessly had things to do. Things that didn't involve him.

The food was fresh and hot, except for the fruit, which was cold. Impressive that they were so efficient, as good or better than most high end hotels and without electricity.

Lost in his own thoughts, he didn't hear Camille's father come into the room. Instead of filling his plate, however, the man sat across from him.

Bradley set down his fork and swallowed what had heretofore been a good bite of egg.

"I'm Camille's father," he said.

"Yes sir. I know."

"My name is Adam Lefleur."

"I'm Bradley Becquerel."

"I know."

Bradley wasn't sure what was expected of him. The man stared into his eyes. Bradley tore his gaze free. This was Camille's father. He needed this man's permission to continue to see her, much less remain in their house.

"Camille tells me you know her from finishing school. That you met at Mass."

"Yes sir." Was the lie more costly when it involved a church?

"Who introduced you?" he asked.

"I don't remember. I was too dazzled by your daughter, Sir."

"So you tracked her here?" Adam asked, ignoring the compliment to his daughter.

"Not at all, Sir. I was in the area on business and stumbled upon Camille by accident. It was fortuitous." No lies this time.

"You're on a first name basis with my daughter?"

Bradley choked back a laugh at the smoke that seemed to come from Adam's ears.

"Miss Lafluer," he quickly corrected. So many things to remember. He could only hope he didn't get himself killed by not knowing the customs.

"You seem to be rather close to my daughter."

"I um." How was he supposed to proceed? "I would like to call upon Miss Lafleur."

Adam scowled. "How do you expect to call upon her when you're sleeping down the hall in the guest room?"

"That's a good question." Perhaps he should have gone about this from a different angle. Camille had mentioned that she was working on an idea.

"You seem to be down on your luck."

"Ha. Yes. I have fallen on some bad luck."

Adam continued to watch him, his brow creased. "Very well," he said. "You can stay in the guest room for the time being. We'll figure the rest out when you're a little less confused," he said, standing up, and pushing his chair forward.

Bradley gaped at the older man as he left the room. He looked down at his plate – at the cold food, and shoved it aside. He'd lost his appetite anyway.

As he sat there, contemplating his next move, Camille

breezed into the room. She was wearing a light blue gown and her hair fell loosely onto her shoulders.

"My father wants to speak to you," she said, breathlessly.

"He was just here."

"Oh dear," she said and dropped to a chair next to him. "I told him you were disoriented from your travels."

"Disoriented. That seems accurate."

"You're still here, so I guess it didn't go too badly."

He shook his head. "I need to go."

"Yes, I know. You need to go get your money."

"I can't be destitute."

"I've arranged for us to visit Madame Laveau at Midnight tonight," she said.

"How did you do that?"

"I have my ways," Camille said, smiling sweetly.

"No, really, how do you know her?"

Camille stood up and went to the window. "She's a hair dresser."

"Your hairdresser?"

Camille shrugged and turned back to face him. "She'd done my hair in the past. When I went to the balls. It's been about a year though since I've gone, so I haven't seen her lately."

"I didn't know that," Bradley said, glancing toward the window. He had no watch, so already he was looking to the sun in order to estimate the time of day. He glanced around, but there were no clocks in this room.

"How would you know?" she asked, scrunching up her face. "Only a few people know her. I heard she used to be active in the Catholic church, but now that she's much older, she only works with a few people."

"She practices voodoo?"

"I don't know. I think she's a healer. But, again, I know her mostly from doing my hair. She's quite good. And she's a good listener."

A few seconds later, the sounds of a grandfather clock drifted through the air and he was instantly reminded of his grandfather's plantation house with the grandfather clock standing in the foyer. Although the kitchen had burned, the house had been saved by the local fire department's quick arrival and valiant efforts.

Thoughts of the house, as always, led to thoughts of his sister. Erika. He had a sudden overwhelming desire to see her. Though he missed her terribly, the thought that she could be here, in 1838 was surreal.

But in order to travel, he would need money. His thoughts had come back full circle to the coins left in his hotel room. He groaned.

"You are in pain?" Camille asked, watching him closely.

"No," he shook his head. "It's just frustrating. I'm here, with you, and, yet, all I can think about is the money that I inadvertently left behind. The money that would give me independence."

He noticed the little flush that spread over her cheeks at his words. She, however, choose to divert the topic. "My father says money is the root of all evil."

Bradley scoffed. "I don't disagree. Unfortunately, it's a necessary evil."

"Very well," she said, with a decisiveness to her tone. "You go get your money and we'll do what it is that we want to do."

He grinned at her, enjoying her change of conversation. "And what is it that we want to do?"

This time, there was no mistaking the flush on her cheeks. "We, um." She looked away. "We need to think of a better reason for you to be here."

"A better reason than the allure of a pretty girl?"

"You, sir, are a rogue."

"Yes, I'm afraid you've found me out."

"Do you not have a lady in your time?"

He shook his head. "I've never met anyone whom I fancied."

"Did you look?"

"I looked in every matchbook and every tinderbox."

"Those are odd places to look for anyone, even a lady," she said, she said her brow furrowed. "That may explain your lack of success."

He laughed. "That's kind of what I thought."

"But that's where you look for potential suitors in your time? We must endure interminable balls."

"I thought young ladies enjoyed going to balls. You don't like dancing?"

"I love to dance. But there are so many elderly widowers that my father would have me wed." She wrinkled her nose.

"Your father would have you wed a widower?" The very thought sickened Bradley.

"He's under the impression that I need a man to take care of me. A man of means."

"Ah ha!"

"What?"

"Ah ha, it's important that you hook up with a man of means."

"It's important to my father that I marry a man of means. Not to me. My family has plenty of money. And I can take care of myself. I can mix drinks and I can keep books. Besides, when I do get married, I want to marry someone I like. Not someone who smells badly."

"Does your father really care who you marry?"

She stretched out her arms, adjusted the lace on her sleeves at her wrists. "I don't know. I love it here at the townhouse. The plantation is ok, but I prefer the excitement of the city. Marriage would mean I would be tucked away taking care of babies."

"Would that be so bad?"

She stood up, walked to the window, looked outside. "No. I

don't know. There's so much to see. I want to travel the country."

Bradley nearly came undone. Here stood the perfect woman for him. A woman who wanted to travel and see the country. If only.

If only he could take her home with him. As a pilot, he had the means to show her the country. He could show her things so far outside of her imagination, it was impossible to fathom.

Perhaps he'd sensed that kindred spirit about her from the beginning. Perhaps that was one of the things that had drawn him to her in the first place. That free-spiritedness.

That and her unparalleled beauty. Perhaps it was from a pureness that could only come from not eating pizza and hamburgers, but her eyes were bright, her skin flawless. Her lips full.

Bradley squirmed in his chair and pulled his eyes away from her straight back and her long, lush hair. He, too, stood up, but instead of following her to the window, he went to the sideboard and, picking up a handful of strawberries, redirected his thoughts. One by one, he pulled the stems from the strawberries and ate them, badly needing the distraction.

She turned her gaze from the window onto him. He set the strawberries aside and leaned against the sideboard, his elbows propped on either side. He smiled and hoped he didn't look as wolfish as he felt.

He must not have, because she returned the smile.

He struggled to pick up a strain of their conversation and said the first thing that popped in his head. "You don't want to have babies?"

Her mouth dropped open.

Apparently this wasn't an appropriate conversation to have with a lady. "I'm sorry," he said, running a hand through his hair. "This isn't something we should talk about?"

She glanced behind her out the window, then after her gaze

flitted about the room, she sighed, and looked at him. "I've only talked about it with my mother and my brothers."

"So... do you?" he asked.

"That's kind of an odd question," she said, going back to sit in her chair. "It's just something that happens when people get married."

Bradley had never thought about it that way. In his world, whether or not to have children was a choice. But in this time period, she was right. It was what happened when people got married... or had intimate relations.

"So, I know you don't want to marry an old man, but do you want to marry at all?"

She gave him another perplexed expression in response. "Things must be much different in your time."

He scoffed. "I can't even begin to explain it. You'd think everyone heathens."

"Are they?"

Bradley considered the question. Some people would, doubtlessly, answer yes. He believed that most people were intrinsically good. By the standards of 1838, however, they would probably appear less than civilized. Bikinis and speedos on beaches. Women in shorts and yoga pants. Premarital sex. Hooking up. "The people are similar," he decided. "But the customs are different."

"Would I like it?" she asked, her eyes bright with anticipation.

He thought about her independence. Her desire to work in the tavern and keep books. Her wish to see the country. He smiled broadly. "Yes," he said. "I think you would like it very much."

A clock somewhere tolled the hour again. He shoved off the sideboard and crossed the space separating them. He held out his hand, palm up, hoping against hope that the movies had gotten it right. She immediately put her hand in his. He kissed the back of her hand. "I must go," he said, "but God-willing, I will soon return."

He turned on his heel and went into the hallway, moving instinctively toward the stairway. His mind began racing. Perhaps he should change back into his jeans before returning to his own time. He glanced down at the jacket and trousers he wore. It was New Orleans, after all. He shouldn't stand out too badly.

The tavern was empty. Someone had turned all the chairs upside down on the tables, presumably to sweep and mop the floors. He hurried across the room, dodging chairs and tables.

He reached out, put a hand on the doorknob, and took a deep breath. Waited. It had been difficult to get back here last time. Would it be more difficult each time?

I just need to get the money and come right back. I won't go anywhere near this door without the money again.

He turned the knob and pushed open the door.

He had to grab hold of the door keep his knees from buckling.

CHAPTER 8

*C*amille watched him walk out the door. The feel of his lips on her hand was still strong. His scent of spice and something unfamiliar still lingered in the room. She turned back to the window and, pushing open the shutters, leaned forward so she could see the front door to the tavern below. When Bradley stepped out, she'd see him.

As the seconds continued to pass, her heart tripped up a notch. Had he made it? Perhaps Madame Laveau had been mistaken. Perhaps it was easier than she had believed to travel back and forth through time.

She was about to lean back and follow him downstairs when she spotted him stepping into the street, nearly in front of a horse and buggy. As he gazed around, her heart went out to him. He was here – lost in time.

And she was the only one who could help him.

Though it created an odd sensation in her stomach, she also thought she may be the reason he was here.

Madame Laveau hadn't said that outright, but something in her expression had led Camille to think of that as a possibility. Perhaps tonight when the fortune-teller met Bradley she would be willing to say more.

Camille fought the urge to go to Bradley. To comfort him. To help him figure out that he may never return to his time. But in her heart, she knew this was something he had to work out for himself. It was something he had to do. She couldn't do it for him. As much as she wanted to.

Steeling herself, she leaned back inside and pulled the shutter closed. She needed to work on the day's accounting.

THOUGH IT WAS ONLY MID-MORNING, THE STREET WAS ALREADY busy. A horse and buggy passed in front of him and another was close behind. These weren't tourist carriages and the road was unpaved. It was the same as it had been yesterday.

He stood just outside the door, at the edge of the street and gazed around him. It was the same, yet, so very different.

It was not a trick of the light or a movie set. There were no cameras. No electric anything. This was 1838. He'd known it before, but his mind still struggled to wrap itself around the idea.

He turned toward the river. Spellbound.

When he came to the Cathedral, he went up the steps, and wandered inside. Once inside, familiarity washed over him. There were only two other people inside – women – kneeling, deep in prayer. He made the sign of the cross before walking down the aisle and genuflected when he reached the altar.

At first his thoughts raced so much he couldn't think. His mind was essentially blank. Then a peacefulness began to settle over him.

This is where he had chosen to be. He had worked hard to get here. But for whatever reason, everything had not gone as planned. Nonetheless, it was a miracle that he was here. He had done it. He had traveled back in time.

His thoughts shifted to Camille. Had she somehow lured him back? Then a horrific thought came to him out of nowhere. Perhaps it wasn't Camille at all. Perhaps she was just an illusion of a reason. Perhaps it was his sister who needed him.

His heart in his throat, he lowered his head and prayed with all his heart. He prayed for many things, but mostly he prayed that his sister was well.

As he knelt, intent on his commune with God, he felt someone kneel next to him. Slowly, he lifted his head and peeked from the corner of his eyes to see who knelt so close to him.

It was a priest. The priest watched him and smiled when Bradley turned to look at him.

"My son," the priest said. "Is there something troubling you that perhaps you'd like to talk about?"

Bradley had never known a priest to be so forthcoming with assistance. The priests of his time stayed away unless approached. He supposed they were trained not to be intrusive.

When Bradley didn't answer, the priest continued. "I don't mean to pry, but you seem to be troubled."

"I am troubled," he admitted.

"I've been told I'm a good listener."

"It's complicated."

"Most troubles are, my son."

Bradley rubbed his eyes. Without opening them, he blurted. "I've found myself somewhere I thought I wanted to be, but now that I'm here, I don't know how it happened and I don't know what I'm supposed to do next."

"That does sound complicated." The priest sat quietly a moment, then continued. "Does it really matter how it happened? Since it got you where you wanted."

Bradley slowly shook his head. "Probably not."

"The priest nodded. "It seems important for you to figure out what to do next."

"I have to do something."

"Maybe. Or maybe time will sort things out."

Bradley chuckled. "Time is the problem."

"Ah. Time is something no one can control."

Bradley looked back at the priest's kindly face. "Has time ever been known to... trifle with people?"

"Ah. Time is fickle. You never know where it goes. Sometimes, it seems to outstay its welcome and other times it's fleeting. Here one moment. Gone the next. No man can get a handle on time. It does what it pleases. If it wants to trifle with someone, I suppose nothing can stop it."

"That's not very comforting."

The priest chuckled. "Perhaps not. But it can also be freeing."

Bradley lowered his eyes again and the priest rested his chin on his hands in silent prayer. "There's a lady involved?" he asked.

Bradley jerked his head up. "What makes you ask that?" he asked, then quickly added. "Father."

The priest chuckled again. "There's usually a lady involved when a man is so troubled as you seem to be."

The priest stood and placed a hand on Bradley's head. "May God be with you, my son," he said and walked away, his robes silently flowing around him.

Bradley exhaled deeply. He was relieved that the priest had left him because he so badly wanted to tell someone about his experiences. And he so very didn't dare. Camille was the only person in this time he could speak to about it. And that had come about quite fortuitously when she had watched him disappear.

He sat a little longer, letting his mind wander as it would, allowing himself to think of nothing in particular.

As he sat there in the coolness of the church's serenity, he realized what his first order of business was.

He had to find his sister.

. . .

HE WANDERED ABOUT THE CITY A BIT MORE, RACKING HIS BRAIN over what he could do for income – just case he was stuck here without his money. Unsuccessful in coming up with anything, he made his way back to Camille's townhouse. Although he expected the door to the tavern to be unlocked, he found it a little disconcerting that he could so freely wander upstairs to the living quarters.

Some of his anxiety about the unlocked door, however, was relieved when he was acknowledged by Billy, the large black man who lurked about the halls. It would be unlikely that anyone unauthorized would get past the man.

He stopped by the dining area first, where he found platters with cornbread, turkey, cheese, and dried apples. Not being the mood for any surprise visitors, he took his plate down the hall to his guest room. He discovered that the window overlooking the courtyard below was actually a door. Delighted with the discovery, he took his plate to the balcony and ate at the little iron table and chair he found there.

It wouldn't be long before it would be too hot to step outside, much less enjoy lunch outdoors. Perhaps tomorrow he could have lunch in the courtyard with Camille. There was a larger version of the table with four chairs nestled beneath a tree in the courtyard.

He'd given a lot of thought to the patterns of his time-travel. He had always traveled back at dusk with the setting sun, then returned after dark. Tonight he would recreate the conditions by having a drink in the tavern, then walking through the door or what he had come to think of as the portal. He smiled to himself at the sci-fi term he'd given to a door in 1838. Assuming that worked, he could get his money and begin the process of traveling back.

If it didn't work, well… he would go to see Madame Laveau

with Camille tonight at Midnight, then begin figuring out a way to get to Natchez to look for his sister.

A knock on his door jarred him from his thoughts and sent him back inside the room. "Yes?" he called.

Marcus opened the door. "Mister Adam would like to call upon you," the servant said.

"Okay," Bradley said, eliciting a raised eyebrow from the other man.

Adam came inside the room. "Bradley. You don't mind if we speak for a moment, do you?"

"Of course not." It wasn't like he had a choice.

"I won't keep you long. I just wanted to add something to our conversation this morning."

Bradley nodded. "Would you like to sit?"

"No, I won't be long. My daughter is very trusting. And she's taken a liking to you. I think she misses the company of her brothers."

"I agree," Bradley said.

Adam didn't appear to hear him. "I'm sure that once you have your feet back under you, you'll be on your way. I understand that a hardship can be personal in nature. Nonetheless, I have eyes throughout the house. You mustn't take advantage of being here in my home with my daughter."

"I would never, Sir. I – "

Adam waved him off. "Words flow freely. It's actions that are important to me. If I have any reason to doubt your sincerity, I'll have you on the streets."

"Yes sir."

Adam was gone as quickly as he had come. Bradley, however, was left feeling edgy. And all the more determined to get the money he had left in his hotel room. It was obvious that his days of being welcome here were limited. No matter what Camille might believe, he couldn't stay here long.

. . .

CAMILLE CLOSED THE LEDGER WITH A SIGH. SHE WAS CAUGHT UP on her bookkeeping. She locked the money away in the strongbox. The membership fee had worked well, but they also did well with nightly walk-in sales. She would talk to her father about implementing two levels. One elite level that required a membership fee and another level for walk-ins and people who didn't or couldn't pay the membership fee. They could build up half the room and add a railing to separate the member area.

Pleased with her idea, she went upstairs to the dining area to eat lunch. For the hundredth time today, she wondered where Bradley was and what he was doing. She worried that he was lost in the city or had come to some harm. She should have gone with him. She would have, but she knew from her brothers that men were proud and needed to do things on their own. They didn't like having a woman taking care of them.

She sighed. Thought of her mother and how she took care of the men in the family. Men were such odd creatures.

She would give him until after her nap. Then she would seek him out and hope that he would accept her help. He seemed agreeable enough. He reminded her of her brothers. Once they got over their little independent streak about something, they were good about talking to her and accepting her thoughts.

Camille woke refreshed from her nap and decided on a dark navy gown for tonight. She thought it best to wear dark clothing when she went out after dark in order to not draw attention to herself. She rang for her lady's maid, Lizette, to help her fasten the gown and to do her hair. Lizette used a hot iron from the fireplace to put loose ringlets in Camille's hair.

"Are you going out tonight, Miss?" Lizette asked.

"Not really," Camille said. When she went out alone, she didn't want anyone to know. Servants gossiped. It was human nature and she didn't hold it against them. She also knew that despite her attentions to be stealthy, she would doubtless be spotted by a servant anyway. But the less information they had about her whereabouts when she went to see Madam Laveau, the better. Her father would be unnecessarily worried if he knew his daughter was going to meet with a voodoo priestess. At least tonight, she, hopefully, wouldn't be alone.

She closed her eyes as Lizette twirled her hair and wove a dark navy ribbon in with the curls. She was looking forward to spending the evening with Bradley. She refused to think that he wouldn't be there. He wasn't daft enough to get lost in the city. Besides, he had no money. And even though he thought he would be going back to his time soon, Camille didn't think so.

After Lizette finished her hair, Camille twirled in front of the mirror. As she walked toward the hallway, she remembered that Bradley wasn't her brother and it wouldn't be proper for her to knock on his door.

"Lizette," she said. "Would you ask Marcus to have Bradley meet me in the dining area?"

"Of course, Miss," Lizette agreed and swiftly went to locate Marcus. Camille sighed. She couldn't send Lizette to his room either. She had no doubt that every servant in the house knew about Bradley. In fact, word had probably traveled all the way to the planation by now.

She made her way to the dining area and stood with her back to the room, watching the people hurry to and fro on the street below.

"Miss Lafleur?" She turned at the sound of Bradley's voice. And smiled broadly.

Though he returned her smiled, he watched her... warily?

"I thought we could eat something, then sit in the tavern until it's time to go to Madame Laveau's."

"Sure," he said, but made no move to approach her. Something was different about him. He seemed more distant.

"Very well," she said, forcing a lightness to her voice that she didn't feel. "What would you like?"

"You don't eat together," Bradley observed to himself.

"What?" she asked, determined to keep the smile on her face.

"You never sit at the table for a meal." He swept a hand down the length of the table that would easily seat eight people.

"Oh. Of course we do. When my mother is here. She insists that we eat together. Especially when my brothers are home. But my father and I see no need. We're busy with our own schedules. It's easier this way."

"Hmm."

"What did you do today?" she asked, moving to the sideboard and picking up a plate. Tonight was fried chicken with okra and tomatoes. There were also apple fritters. Since Bradley made no move to join her, she filled a plate and set it on the table. "Here," she said. "Everything the cook makes is wonderful. I think she must especially like fried foods, though, because she never fails to outdo herself." While she talked, she filled a second plate and set it across the table from the first.

"If you aren't going to talk to me, the least you can do is eat with me," she said, smiling sweetly.

He moved to the chair and sat. Instead of looking at the food, he kept his eyes on her. "You look beautiful," he said, his voice barely a whisper.

"Thank you for the compliment," she said, taking a small bite of chicken. "But you're acting strangely."

"My apologies," he said, shaking his head. "Your father came to see me."

"Oh no. Again?" she said. "What did he say to you now?"

"Nothing much," Bradley said. "He merely reinforced the importance of me finding a way to make it on my own here in this time."

"And you will," she said, her smile turning to determination. "I already have something in mind, but I don't want to talk to you about it yet, until we see what happens tonight," she said, with a quick glance toward the door.

Bradley tasted the chicken. "This is excellent," he said.

"I know. We have the best cook."

They ate in silence for a few minutes.

"Are you still planning to try to get your money tonight?" she asked.

"I have to. I have to at least try."

"Very well. Either way, I'm going to see Madame Laveau."

"Is it safe for you to go alone?"

"Probably not, but I'll do it anyway. I've gone alone before."

"Why not take one of the servants?"

"The servants won't go near her. They're convinced that they won't live long enough to make it home."

"But you aren't afraid of her?"

"She's never threatened me. She'd always been quite pleasant."

After they finished eating, they went downstairs to the tavern. After they settled in at her favorite table near the back of the room, and each had a glass of wine, she told him about her idea for the membership levels.

"MISS LAFLEUR, YOU ARE BRILLIANT," BRADLEY SAID. AGAIN, HE was convinced that she was a modern twenty-first century woman stuck in 1838. He needed to find a way to bring her back to the future with him. It was unfortunate that it wasn't possible. He shook his head.

"Why do you shake your head?" she asked.

"I believe you're ahead of your time," he said.

"Nonsense. Every woman has to take care of her household. It's what we're trained to do. Taking care of the tavern is no different."

"But it is different. Growing a business like this is what half the women of the future dream about doing. They go to school to learn how to do what you just naturally figure out all on your own."

"What do your men do?"

"Ha. Our men do what men have always done. We take care of our families and fight for our country."

"So if women are growing businesses and men are working, women and men are equals?" She smiled brightly.

"We're working on it," he said. "There are still a few snags to work out, but we're getting there."

"You wouldn't think it would take so very long."

"You're right. You wouldn't."

It was growing dark now and Bradley was feeling the urge to step through that door. "I have to step outside for a minute."

Her eyes darkened and she lowered her head.

"I'll be back," he assured her.

She lifted her gaze to his, her eyes haunted. "You don't know that."

He held out his hand, his palm up. She put her hand in his and he wrapped his fingers around hers and held tightly. "Do you trust me?" he asked.

"I trust you. I don't trust the Gods or whatever force it is that determines whether or not you move about through time."

"Whatever it is, surely it wouldn't be so cruel as to bring us together only to keep us apart for eternity."

"You, Mister Becquerel have more faith in such things than I do."

He lifted her hand and pressed his lips lightly on the back of her hand. "I will see you shortly," he said.

Quickly, before he could change his mind, he stood up and crossed the room. *I won't look back.*

He looked back at her, though, anyway, through the haze of the cigar smoke. She was lovely. So young. So elegant. So brilliant.

And he knew his heart wasn't in this. He knew she was right. He could step through that door and never come back here. It could be merely a cruel twist of fate that brought them together for a short time.

He turned back, opened the door, and stepped through.

He turned his face to the sky and laughed as a host of conflicting emotions rushed through him. Relief. Disappointment. Disbelief. Resignation.

He looked up and down the street, illuminated only by moonlight. A chicken fluttered at his feet, pecking at something in the dirt. A rider on horseback dismounted and secured his horse on the hitching post next to where Bradley stood.

There were no drunken revelers. No street lights. No cars.

He was still here in 1838.

He pivoted, went back inside and crossed the room to their table where Camille sat patiently waiting, her expression blank. He picked up his glass of wine, drained it, and said. "I didn't finish my drink."

He then headed back to the door, opened it without hesitation, and walked outside.

The chicken had only moved about three feet.

This time he did feel the disappointment wash over him as reality began to settle in. He walked the few feet to the front of the hotel and, sitting on a bench, put his head in his hands.

The worst part of the whole thing was facing Camille. She'd warned him that he would be staying here, but he hadn't believed her. He had been determined to be right about this.

He straightened and leaned back on the bench. A few minutes later, Camille came toward him. She wore a dark hooded cloak, her hands buried in its pockets.

"Let's go," she said.

Wordlessly, he stood up and followed her down the street

and left down an alleyway. As they moved toward the river, Camille kept her eyes straight ahead, her intent unwavering.

Bradley, on the other hand, could not help looking all around him. The mist from the river created tendrils of fog as they neared the river.

When she reached a row of small houses, she went straight up to the one with a green door and knocked. Standing next to her, his hands in his pockets, he wondered if they should go. It was growing cold and there were shadows in the mist.

Camille glanced at him, an eyebrow defiantly raised, so he said nothing.

A few minutes later, a small woman dressed in black lace from head to toe opened the door and stepped aside for them to enter. "You brought your young man, Bradley," she said.

Camille gasped, "I didn't tell you his name."

"You didn't have to. Madam Laveau knows all."

A shiver ran along Bradley's spine. She couldn't possibly know his name.

Camille frowned at the woman. Bradley shifted from one foot to the other as he remembered the old song about the voodoo priestess. *Please don't anger her.*

"Come," the older woman said, "Let's sit."

Camille and Bradley sat next to each other on the couch. There were candles burning on the end tables, and the coffee table. A large sleek black cat lounged on the coffee table, amidst the burning candles. Bradley could only think of the fire hazard. His mother would have never had an open flame with her cats about.

"You want to know when you can return to your own time."

Bradley swallowed a healthy gulp of skepticism and nodded. "Yes."

"It will be sometime," she said.

"How do you know this?" Bradley asked.

"Why I know things isn't important." Her eyes were dark,

both the color and the area around her eyes – smudged with what looked like eyeliner or maybe just coal.

"What am I supposed to do here?" he asked.

Madame Laveau smiled broadly. "You have much to do here."

"I don't understand how I'm supposed to know."

"You have two women to deal with in this time. Surely they are more important than your busy schedule in the future."

Bradley stared at the woman. And promptly shuttered his emotions.

Camille glanced at him. She did not look pleased.

"There is only Camille," he said.

"Two women," the older woman insisted. "Three if you count your grandmother."

Now Bradley knew the woman was pulling threads. Threads that may or may not be true. It's what fortune tellers did. He grinned smugly. He had found her out.

"Vaughn is not dead," Madame Laveau said.

Bradley nearly toppled off the couch.

The voodoo priestess closed her eyes and lifted her eyes toward the ceiling. "She calls to you," she said. "She wants to see you."

Bradley held his breath. What did this woman truly know?

"Before it's too late," she continued.

"My grandmother is already dead," he said.

"When a person goes missing, there are many reasons why a body isn't found. Perhaps they are dumped in the river. Or perhaps they walked through a rip in time."

Bradley kept his eyes on the woman. This was too much. He didn't know how she knew what she knew, but it was beginning to make him uncomfortable.

Beyond beginning. He needed to get out of there. He stood up.

"Wait," Camille said, holding a hand out toward Bradley, but keeping her eyes on the fortuneteller. "How can he find her?"

"His grandmother is the woman I spoke to you about last time. Her name is Vaughn."

Camille cut her eyes toward Bradley.

What was going on? What did Camille and this woman know about his grandmother, Vaughn? "I'll be outside," he said, ignoring Camille's outstretched hand and stepping outside to gulp in the the fresh night air. He'd thought he was going to suffocate when he heard her speak of his grandmother.

There were any number of ways the woman could have known his name. Servants gossiped and since they knew Camille had a guest, someone could have easily found out his name.

But no one, no one, should have known Vaughn's name. There was no Internet. This is 1838. Vaughn had been born years from now.

This was impossible. He paced a few feet away. Stared at nothing. Paced back.

What was it his grandfather had said? *She was born in the 1700s. She had just gotten to America when she was attacked by Indians. Somehow her life was saved and she ended up in the 1800s.*

Camille needed to get away from that woman. The woman was a witch.

He saw a shadow out of the corner of his eye, turned, but nothing was there. This happened several more times and he was about to jump out of his skin. He was beginning to wonder which was worse, being out here alone in the fog with the shadows that may or may not be anything or inside with the witch.

Finally, after what seemed like forever, Camille came out of the woman's house. Her face was flushed and her eyes were bright.

"We need to get out of here," he said.

"I was only a minute," she said.

"A minute my… foot. You were in there forever."

"Are you afraid of the fog?" she asked, pulling her hood over her head.

"Not the fog. But what's in it."

She glanced around. Started to say something, but one of the shadows passed directly in front of them. "Yes, we should go home," she said.

As they hurried down the dark alleyway in the fog, Bradley took her hand and hoped he was going the right way. Now that they had some distance between them and Madame Laveau, he slowed down. Her hand was small and delicate in his.

The moon was only a sliver mostly hidden behind the clouds.

"Are we going the right way?" Bradley asked.

"We're sort of taking the scenic route. But I don't mind. It's a safer area here." They came to the end of the block. "Turn right here."

They went around to the courtyard and sat at the little iron table before going back inside.

"I don't think we should go back there again," Bradley said.

"I agree."

"What did she tell you after I left?"

She turned away. "Nothing really," she said. "Something about me bringing you here to see her. I guess she knew you didn't want to be here."

But he could tell she was lying. Madame Laveau had given Camille some more information while he was out of earshot.

I have to get away from here, Bradley thought again. *I have to find my sister.*

CHAPTER 9

Camille locked the strongbox. *It's only temporary,* she reminded herself. *If she put the money back, it wasn't stealing.* Besides, she'd never taken any payment for any of the work she'd done for her father. She didn't need it. She had everything she needed.

Still, despite her justification, she felt guilty about borrowing the money. *I'll go to confession.*

The bag of coins was heavy. Nonetheless, she tucked it into her skirt pocket. She glanced around the office. Everything was caught up and tidied away.

The timing could not have been better. Her father had gone to the plantation to visit with her mother would not be back for another two weeks. Perhaps she would even be back before he returned.

David would collect the money and keep up with it while she was away. He had a key to a small lockbox where they kept money for incidentals. She would tell him she was going to be away for a few days. There was certainly to need to give him specifics. He would assume she was joining her parents at the plantation. No one needed to know that she would actually be staying on the boat, past her parents' plantation up the river, and travelling to Natchez.

It occurred to her, however, that she should leave a note for her father. Just in case. They would be traveling by riverboat which was not always the safest mode of travel.

She pulled out a sheet of paper and penned a letter to her father.

Dear Father,

In case I'm not back by the time you return, please do not be distressed. I had to travel unexpectedly to Natchez in order to help locate Mr. Becquerel's sister.

Your loving daughter,

Camille

She reread the note, then ripped it up and tossed it into the fireplace. Her father would kill her for traveling unchaperoned with a man. In fact, if anyone found out that Bradley was anything other than her cousin, her reputation would be destroyed. Her father would be furious.

She should be back before two weeks were up anyway. No need to risk her father's ire.

She went upstairs to her room and made some final changes to her trunk. She had packed pretty much her whole spring wardrobe along with her shawl and cloak. The weather this time of year was unpredictable.

She needed to check on Bradley to see if he needed any help with figuring out what to pack. It was mid-morning, so she decided to risk going to the guest room. Moving unnoticed, she made her way to his door and knocked lightly. He didn't answer.

She heard someone coming up the stairs, so to avoid being discovered, she opened the door and slipped inside, keeping her eyes down and her back to the room. "Bradley?" she asked.

"You can turn around," he answered, with amusement in his voice.

She turned around, keeping her back against the door. And giggled. He had clothes strewn all over the bed.

He shrugged. "I travel all the time, but I have no idea what I'm supposed to take."

"Would you like me to help?" she asked.

"Please. I don't even know what goes with what."

She went to the opened trunk and peaked inside. It was empty. She giggled again.

"I'm glad you find this humorous."

"I can help you," she said, and began sorting trousers, shirts, jackets, socks, and cravats. She glanced at him sideways. He'd been wearing the same outfit she had picked out for him two days ago. She'd changed clothes half a dozen times.

"How often do you wash your clothes?" he asked.

If anyone else had asked her that, she would have thought they were jesting or daft. She knew, however, that Bradley seriously didn't know how things worked around here.

"The servants take care of it," she explained as she sorted and placed things into the trunk. "They can't wash the wool, but they can brush off dirt and stains. They air it out. That's why we wear the cotton undergarments. You can wear those a couple of days depending on how hot it gets. They wash the undergarments in hot, soapy water, then hang them to dry."

"That makes sense," he said. "You don't have to come with me," he said, for the tenth time since they'd begun to plan this trip.

"Don't be silly. You'd be lost as a goose."

He nodded. "You're right. I'm glad you're going with me."

"Just remember," she said. "you're my cousin."

"Got it."

BRADLEY HAD UNDERSTOOD IMMEDIATELY WHEN CAMILLE HAD told him about the necessity of them traveling as cousins. In a world where her reputation could be ruined just for stopping by his room or touching his hand in public, he was surprised she was even allowed to travel with him as cousins.

But then the key thing was that her father didn't even know she was going.

"Did you get the money?" he asked.

She nodded. "I think it'll be enough. I don't pay much attention to what things cost."

Such was the life of the wealthy southern belle. Another reminder that he could never be good enough for her in her time period. In the future, he would stand a chance.

He wondered how long they would be gone. She had said they had two weeks while her father was at their plantation up the river. She'd promised to point it out to him as they passed by on their way to Natchez.

That meant two weeks before he would have the opportunity to walk through the portal again. There was, of course, no way to know, but he had an unsubstantiated gut feeling that the longer he waited, the less likely it would be that he could travel through time again.

He was about to come out of his skin in eager anticipation at seeing his sister again and talking to her about all this time-travel stuff. She had doubtlessly developed her own theories about how it worked. Then again, she was less analytic than he was. Bradley was the one who looked for patterns in everything – the weather, people. Erika tended to just go with her emotions. He wondered what she was doing in this time period. Would she be working as a veterinarian or would she have children? The thought of his sister having a child gave him a weird feeling.

"Bradley," he heard his name called with impatience.

"Sorry. What?"

"I asked which color cravat you prefer."

"They look about the same to me," He smiled with the fact that she had called him by his first name for the first time.

She was holding up a maroon color and a slightly lighter maroon color cravat.

"We'll take both," she said, dropping them into the trunk.

"You think like I do," he said. He watched her with open admiration. Though he'd been distracted by the whole time-travel thing, she was still the most beautiful woman he'd ever seen.

They were becoming better acquainted with each other and he'd discovered that he not only liked looking at her, but he also enjoyed her company. In truth, that was a rarity. It was especially a problem he'd encountered in dating. He'd go out with a pretty girl, but they'd have nothing to talk about. Or he'd go out with an intelligent, decently attractive woman, but he'd have no desire to kiss her.

He was funny about where he put his lips. Always had been. Some guys would kiss girls they had no attraction to and be okay with it, but not Bradley. He'd rather do without than settle with less than an all-around attraction – body and mind. It probably explained a lot about why he was still single.

"Mr. Becquerel. Your head is somewhere else today," Camille said.

"I'm sorry. I'm distracted, I guess, because I'm excited about getting to see my sister."

"I understand," she said, sitting on the settee. "I'd be so excited I wouldn't be able to sit still if I was on my way to see my brothers."

When they got to the steamboat, there was a line. They had had their trunks sent ahead by one of the servants.

"Is there always a line like this?" Bradley asked, looking

around at the throngs of people, some waiting to board, others obviously just came to watch the boat.

"Sometimes, but I usually have tickets in advance. We could do that and come back tomorrow or the next day if you want to. We could probably get a cabin that way."

"I don't want to wait," he said, glad for the hesitation in her voice. He didn't care if they had to stand all the way to Natchez.

"I don't think we're going to get a cabin," she said, chewing the nail on her little finger.

Bradley looked at the clear sky, with a few puffy clouds. "The weather's clear," he said. "And the temperature is pleasant. We can sit on the deck."

"For two days?"

"Sure. It'll be nice."

She shook her head. "It's going to rain tonight."

He looked askance at her, then back to the sky. "What makes you say that?"

"The air is damp."

Bradley almost opened his mouth to explain that it was humidity and it didn't mean that it was going to rain. It's New Orleans, after all. But, instead, he bit his tongue and decided to let it go. She would have no way to know about such things.

After what seemed like an interminably long wait, they reached the ramp leading to the Oronoko steamboat and found that Camille had been right. There were no cabins left. "You still want to go?" she asked again.

He nodded. "We have to."

After going up the ramp, they climbed the iron stairs to the top deck. Though it was crowded, they were able to find an unoccupied space on one of the benches. "Is there some place to get something to drink?" He was thinking that a bottle of Smart Water would be perfect right now.

"I think so," she said. "If you want to go see, I can save our space."

After he stood up, she spread her skirts around her and did indeed cover the space he'd just vacated. He smiled to himself. There were definitely advantages to wearing hoop skirts with voluminous skirts.

"Wait," she said, before he walked away. "You might need this," she said as she pressed a coin into his hand.

He took the coin, put it in his pocket, then kissed her palm.

Though he regretted leaving her alone even for a moment, he enjoyed the novelty of being among the passengers. Most people seem excited to be there, many of them possibly riding for the first time. He recognized a few seasoned travelers, mostly older, well-dressed men. It was a hazard of his job as a pilot, he supposed, to be able to distinguish those who were accustomed to travel from those who were not.

There were children running about and couples gazing over the rails. Business men with their heads bent together. It was a fascinating thing to witness.

He made his way through the crowd and went below deck. He finally found a wait staff dressed all in white to ask for a drink of water. The man disappeared, then returned a few minutes later with two glasses of water.

"How far are you traveling, Sir?" the waiter asked.

"To Natchez."

"Very good, Sir. You'll be with us for two days then."

"Two days. Seems like a long time."

"Oh, yes sir. We have a lot of stops to make along the way."

"What are we stopping for?"

"We stop for passengers and make deliveries to the plantations."

"So this is a freighter?" He asked, drinking his glass of water in one long pull."

"Yes sir. Let me refill that for you, Sir."

Bradley waited for the man to return with more water. "Where do people sleep who don't have cabins?"

"Oh, passengers sleep all over the place."

Bradley thanked him for the water and started back up to the top deck. By the time he made it back, the ship was well underway. Camille sat where he had left her, her back to the crowd, staring toward the shore.

She turned and smiled when he stood in front of her. "It's crowded," she said, taking the water from him.

"Very. It looks like we'll be sleeping here," he said,

"We'll need to find a place below this afternoon. It's going to rain tonight."

Bradley smiled to himself as he sipped his water, pacing himself this time.

"Does it look like this in your time?" she asked.

Bradley gazed at the banks of the river as they left the city. The river was a mile wide, but the banks were undeveloped. Trees lined the banks where buildings would clutter it in the future. They passed a cluster of small houses, a little community just outside the city, yet in this world, it was so far out, rural even.

"No, it's much prettier now."

"How has it changed?" she asked, curiosity furrowing her brow.

How could he possibly explain it? "There are buildings now, industrial buildings." She frowned. "Large box-like buildings that are used for storage."

"Like a barn?" she asked.

He nodded. "Sort of like a barn, only much, much larger, and unsightly."

"No houses?"

"There are houses. But..." Did he really want to get into electricity? Taking a deep breath, he dove in. "The houses are all connected by wires. The wires are rather ugly."

"Why on earth would all the houses need to be connected?"

"They use something called electricity. The electricity runs through the wires and provides light and energy to all the houses."

She sat quietly a few minutes, seemingly sorting out what he had said.

"Light, like candle light?"

"Yes! Exactly. People actually use candles for decoration in the future."

"Candles are nice. I'm glad people still use them."

The steamboat began slowing and easing toward the right bank. "What are we doing" Bradley asked.

"We must be slowing at a dock."

"Already?"

Camille glanced at him, sideways. "This is a long way out by horseback. The boat is so much faster."

Bradley sipped his water. "I suppose is it." Someday, perhaps, he would explain the concept of air travel. Or perhaps he would keep that to himself. There were some things that would be overwhelming for anyone to comprehend.

As they neared the dock, the steamboat whistle shattered the air. The air was filled with voices, "Four Twain!" Then later "Mark Twain!" They were on the wrong side of the ship to see what was going on. "What are they doing?" he asked.

"They send a yawl to exchange passengers."

"A yawl?"

"A smaller boat. The ship can't get close to the bank."

"I see," Bradley said. No wonder it took two days to go up the river from New Orleans to Natchez.

"What else do you have in your world besides this electric city?"

Bradley chuckled. "We have cell phones."

"What is that?"

An addiction, he thought, fighting the impulse even now to

check his pocket for his. "It's a little box with numbers on it that you can talk to other people with. Each person is assigned their own number. So, you could have your brother's number, key it into your box, and he would pick his box up on the other end and you could talk."

"You must be teasing me!" she said, her eyes wide.

He shook his head and fervently wished he could show her. As he thought about it, cell phones had to be the best invention ever created. "We started with phones in our houses. Then a few years ago, they became portable and people could take then wherever they went."

"I want one," she decided. "Can you make one for me?"

He laughed. "If I could do that, we'd be famous. I wish I could. But it was a very long process involving a lot of people. And things that haven't even been invented yet."

"That's too bad," she pouted. "I would love more than anything to talk to my brothers right now."

"I understand," he said. And he did. Now that they were on the boat on their way to Natchez, he was ready to see his sister. He had no idea how they would find her, but he would cross that bridge when he came to it.

"So you gave up electric cities that don't need candles and cells that you can talk to anyone at any time anywhere."

He nodded. Smiled at her awe.

"What else did you give up?"

He couldn't even begin to list all the things they had in his world. Things to come. Cars. Planes. Computers. Plumbing. Television. Fast food. Medical care.

"Did you give up anything that you can't live without?"

"Medical care, maybe," he murmured.

Her eyes widened. "I can't imagine the advances that must have been made in medical care. Do people still die?"

"Unfortunately, yes. But they do tend to live longer. Unless they're in an accident. Or have an incurable disease."

"Sort of like now."

"Sort of, except that there are things that can be treated in the future that can't be treated now."

"Like what?"

"Well," he lowered his voice. "It's not for a lady's ears, but dysentery."

She nodded, not in the least shocked. "I know several people who have died from that."

"I don't know of anyone who has."

"Goodness. That's progress then." She looked around and must have spotted a landmark that only she could recognize. "We'll be passing my family's plantation soon."

"Really? We'll be able to see it from the river?"

"Oh yes. It's quite visible."

They rounded a bend and the steamboat began heading toward the bank again, this time on their side.

"Oh dear," Camille said.

"What is it?" Bradley asked, all manner of problems entering his imagination. He remembered reading about the frequent steamboat explosions.

"We're going to be slowing at my family's dock."

And sure enough, the boat slowed and veered a little toward the land, the sounder measuring with his leather strap and calling out "Four Twain!" A large white plantation home came into view. As they got closer, Bradley could see that larger was a gross understatement. The house was a large three story mansion surrounded by balconies all around, as well as Greek columns, all shaded by huge oak trees.

A man on a horse waited at the dock, as well as several servants. They had crates waiting to load onto the boat.

Camille ducked behind Bradley. "That's my father," she said.

"I don't think he could recognize you from here."

"I don't want to risk it," she said.

Bradley watched as the servants loaded the crates on the

boat and then returned with other crates. "What's in the crates?" he asked.

Camille glanced toward the bank. "Sugarcane to sell and other various supplies to be dropped off."

Bradley found the whole process fascinating. "Is it a barter system?" he asked.

"Oh no. My father sells his sugar cane and cotton to the highest bidder. He orders supplies from the city or wherever he gets them at the lowest cost possible. He has a lot of mouths to feed."

"Mouths? You mean your family?"

"My family and also the servants. They have their own gardens, but it's not nearly enough for them to be self-sufficient. My father has to make sure they're fed and have clothes to wear."

They traveled in silence for a few minutes. There were dark clouds brewing in the distance.

"We should start looking for a place to spend the night," she said.

"Because of the rain," he said.

She nodded. Smiled. She knew he didn't believe her. By the time they gathered up their things and started to go below desk, a raindrop landed on the back of Bradley's hand. He looked up at the dark clouds and vowed never to doubt Camille again. All his training in the study of meteorology as well as his training in aviation and it had taken someone who didn't even know what the Weather Channel was to predict this rain shower.

It was more difficult to find a space to sit inside, but they managed to find a bench that was empty. The impending darkness was more noticeable below deck.

"I've never traveled without a cabin," she said.

"Not even just to the plantation?"

"Not even," she admitted

"This is a new experience then," he said

"And one I'm not interested in repeating. We should have brought food."

"I can go in search of food." He nodded, looking around. "Other people have food."

"I think they brought it with them, but you can go look."

"I will do that. Will you be alright here?"

"There isn't really anyplace I can go," she said. He could tell the crowdedness and discomfort was beginning to wear on her.

LATER THAT EVENING, AFTER THEY HAD EATEN SOME BREAD AND fried chicken, Camille felt that her eyelids were going to fall closed. She leaned her head back and felt herself nodding off.

Bradley shifted on the bale of cotton they had found to sit on.

He must have apologized about ten times for being the one responsible for her not having a cabin to sleep in, much less a bed.

It's not his fault, she thought, as her head wobbled sleepily.

Bradley shifted again, this time putting his arms around her and guiding her head to his lap. She didn't know where he'd found a pillow, but she was grateful.

She couldn't hold her eyes open any longer and would have fallen asleep standing up if he hadn't been there to save her.

BRADLEY BLAMED HIMSELF. CAMILLE SHOULD NEVER HAVE BEEN on a boat without a cabin to sleep in. She was much too delicate. And, he thought, glancing warily around, it wasn't exactly safe to be out here in the open. Sleeping. Most of what Camille referred to as the refined people were upstairs, either in their cabins or dancing and drinking in the ballroom. He could hear some more boisterous folks laughing and singing on the outside lower deck. He watched another young man pass by, glancing at Camille as he passed. Everyone at least glanced at Camille. She was a siren for men's eyes.

He would have to stay awake while she slept. Resigned to not getting any sleep, he gazed down at the one he vowed to protect.

Her lips were slightly parted in sleep. Her eyelashes were dark smudges against her porcelain skin. He couldn't resist picking up a lock of her long, raven hair. So soft. Every protective instinct he had was on full alert.

He looked around and wondered what he, a pilot, could possibly do if they were attacked. He hoped and prayed that, unlike in the movies, they wouldn't be disturbed.

Leaning his head back against the wall, he took a deep steadying breath. He'd had a few appointments with a psychologist after his sister had gone back in time. Though he'd been supportive, he was left with grief. He'd even told the psychologist that his sister had died. Which, in truth, for him, she had.

The psychologist had guided him through the process of grieving and dealing with the subsequent anxiety. She had given him a prescription for Xanax and taught him to relax. Taught him that anxiety comes from trying to control things that he couldn't control. And truthfully, there was very little anyone could control. It was all an illusion.

At the time, that idea seemed to help him, but right now, he found it depressing.

Shifting his thoughts, he went back to the problem at hand. Camille was the woman for him. He had very little lingering doubt that destiny had put him here to be with her. The problem was finding a way to support her in the manner she was accustomed to. He scoffed. In this world, he was a pauper, and although it was by accident that they were sleeping in a public area on a cotton bale, even if there had been room available, he wouldn't have been able to even afford the smallest of cabins.

It was too soon to tell her how her felt about her. Or was it? She trusted him enough to come on this journey with him. But was it more than trust? Did she feel the love that he felt?

His eyes were heavy. He wasn't sure he was going to make it through the night.

She stirred and opened her eyes, then shifted to sit up. "Do you want to sleep for a little while?" she asked. "I can keep watch and wake you when I get sleepy again."

"You are a God-send," he said, too drowsy to even question how she'd known that he was staying awake to keep watch.

CAMILLE MOVED THE HAVERSACK SHE'D MISTAKEN FOR A PILLOW into her own lap. She patted it for Bradley to put his head in her lap.

"Just for minute," he said. "Wake me up when you start to get sleepy."

"I will," she said, but in truth she was wide awake now. There was so much to think about. She had never travelled without a chaperone and the whole trip was one of the most exciting things she'd ever done. Indeed, it was hard to sit still, when there was so much excitement all around them. Music drifted from the upper deck, where she knew there would be dancing and laughter. There were still a few people walking about, but most who had come below, had come looking for a place to sleep. Other than the occasional passerby, the nearest person was an elderly man asleep on a cotton bale several feet away.

Bradley had instantly fallen asleep when his head hit her lap. He was snoring so very lightly she could barely hear it. She smiled at the notion that she knew that about him. It seemed risqué that she knew so much about a man she wasn't married to.

Her thoughts looped around to one of the things she liked so much about him. Things besides him being handsome and kind. She like it that he wasn't a plantation owner or a tavern owner or an owner of anything. She liked it that he had nothing. He was the one man she had ever met who would not try to take her away from her home and her family.

Camille was nothing if not loyal to home and family. That was the primary reason she remained single at age twenty-two. She'd had ample offers from suitors and both her mother and her father had urged her to find a suitable husband before it was too late. Camille had hoped it was too late. Besides, her brothers were older than she and neither of them had been pressured into taking a wife.

But then there was Bradley. She ran her fingers through his smooth short hair. He looked so… clean compared to the men she was accustomed to. He was most handsome.

As she sat, studying him, allowing her mind to wander freely, she wondered if he was the one who could entice her away from her home.

She sighed with relief that she didn't have to make that choice. She could bring him into her fold, knowing that he had no reason not to stay.

He stopped snoring and stirred. She jerked her hand away from his hair, feeling the flush on her cheeks.

He rolled over and looked up at her with a sleepy smile. "My turn?" he asked.

Her heart seemed to swell and burst in a million tiny little pieces that shot through her all at once. It was more than him not trying to rip her from her family and carry her away with him.

The shards of love that shot through her and the irony of the whole situation brought a bubble of laughter to her lips.

. . .

THEY ALTERNATED THEIR SLEEP CYCLE SEVERAL TIMES OVER THE next few hours. The boat slowed so many times to drop off and pick up passengers and freight that Bradley wondered if they would ever get to Natchez. Though he had no watch, he estimated that a boy went through at least every hour to announce their location in case someone needed to disembark. He didn't recognize most of the stops, probably names of plantations, but he recognized enough to know that they were not even halfway.

He groaned. That meant another night sleeping in the open on cotton bales. At the first signs of light, after Camille opened her eyes, he suggested they go above deck. The rain had moved on leaving the air fresh.

There were several well-dressed families waiting to disembark at the next stop. He left Camille in the breakfast line and went in search of someone in charge. Unable to find anyone, he wandered into the cabin area and located a porter. After a brief discussion, he had secured a small cabin. At least Camille would have a place to sleep tonight. No one seemed to know for sure, but it seemed they would be arriving in Natchez by mid-morning tomorrow.

Half an hour later, they sat on the upper deck in the warm, fresh morning sunshine eating a breakfast of stale biscuits.

"If you want it, you have a cabin for tonight," he said.

She gaped at him. "How did you manage that?"

"I found the right person to ask," he replied with a shrug, though he was secretly pleased that she was excited about it. "I don't know who to pay though."

"Oh," her eyes lit up. "I know the answer to that."

"Then, in that case, we make a good team," he said, catching himself before he held up his hand for a high five.

"I didn't realize it would take this long to get to Natchez," she said.

He nodded. "This trip is interminable. What are we going to do for the rest of the day?" He asked, thinking about modern cruise ships with games, pools, spas, mini-golf, and even sky diving. He'd even go for a movie.

"We can walk about, talk. I brought a book," she said.

He wondered how they were going to walk about with so many people crowding the deck. "I didn't bring a book," he said, wishing for his iPad, loaded with Kindle ebooks. One reason he'd been drawn to aviation was his desire to get from place to place quickly. Family trips in the back seat of the family SUV had been torture for him. His sister could sit and read contently for hours, but Bradley suffered.

"Wouldn't it be lovely if we could just hop onto, I don't know, a wagon, and fly from place to place?" Camille asked.

Bradley's water went down the wrong way and he went into a coughing spell.

"Are you going to live?" she asked.

"I'm not so sure," he said. The woman was a prophet and didn't have a clue.

"Did I say something?"

He held out his hand. She put hers in his and he smiled into her eyes. "Nothing at all, my dear. Nothing at all."

They spent the day waving at people from the deck when the boat veered close enough to send a small boat to the bank to exchange passengers, walking a bit, and talking. By early evening, they sat quietly, reading Camille's book.

AFTER SUPPER, CAMILLE SUGGESTED THAT IT WAS TIME FOR HER to sleep. Bradley immediately agreed, but his heart sank. They hadn't been separated since they got on the boat and the thought of not being at her side caused his heart to sink.

They located her cabin and she reached into her pocket to pull out the key the porter had given her earlier. The porter was truly a miracle worker because he had located their trunks and brought them to the room. He had thought they were married and neither of them had corrected him.

It hadn't hurt that Camille had smiled at him and thanked him profusely.

She put her key in the lock and turned it.

"We should make sure it's good before I leave," he said, his voice a little gravelly even to his own ears.

She nodded and shifted for him to push the door open. It was a small cabin, but it did have a nice window. The bed took up half the space and their trunks most of the other half.

"What do you think?" he asked, turning to gauge her reaction. He was certain it wasn't up to her standards, but it was certainly better than sleeping on a bale of cotton.

She wasn't looking at the room, however, she was gazing at him.

They stood, about a foot apart, gazing at each other. He was mesmerized by her green eyes locked onto his. Her eyes were bright with unshed tears. Her lips were parted slightly.

"What is it?" he asked, closing the distance between them and taking her into a hug. He knew he was breaking every respectable rule possible in this 1830s world, but a distressed damsel was a distressed damsel no matter what the century. Her arms locked around his waist and he held her closer. Her head fit perfectly beneath his chin. A peaceful sense of coming home enveloped him.

He kissed the top of her head and felt her breath hitch. Shifting a bit, he put a finger beneath her chin to tip her face up. A single tear had slipped from her closed eyes. Forgetting everything about propriety, he kissed it away.

Then he held her close again, restraining from kissing her on the mouth. From kissing those luscious pink lips.

As they stood there, he watched the deepening colors of the sunset and the subsequent darkening of the room. He'd read enough to know that he needed to leave her. Every moment he stayed, he increased the risk of ruining her reputation.

He pulled back. "I have to go," he said, sliding his hands down her arms to take her hands in his.

Her head still down, she nodded. Then she lifted her chin and met his eyes again. "I don't want you to go," she whispered.

"But, my love, you know I can't stay."

"I can't stand the thought of you out there. Alone." She pulled away and swept a hand around the room. "Besides, who would know?"

"We would," he replied, feeling that sense of protectiveness toward her – even from himself.

She looked from the bed to the trunks. "There are two pillows and two blankets." She turned her attention back to him. "But I suppose a cotton bale would be more comfortable than the floor."

"What are you suggesting?" he asked, feeling a surge of hope that he didn't dare overly entertain.

"You could take the extra linens and sleep on the floor."

He nodded. "I don't know if that would be proper."

She scoffed. "Is it proper for me, your charge, to allow you to sleep out there in the open on a cotton bale while I sleep here, in a bed, behind a closed door?"

"Yes," he said, but the sense of hope grew.

"Nonsense," she said, going to the bed and pulling a pillow from it "I won't allow it. You're my guest and I would be remiss in allowing you to take such a risk. You don't know the customs and one misstep could put you in danger."

He caught the pillow that she tossed to him and smiled. "You're most persuasive," he said. And, yes, he would rather sleep on a hard cold floor any day next to her than on the relative comfort of a cotton bale. Which wasn't as soft as he had imagined. In fact, he wondered if it was not as rough as any floor.

"We have to do a bit of rearranging first," he said, handing her pillow back. He slid both trunks to the middle of the floor, leaving just enough room on the other side for him. Standing with the trunks between them, he reached for the pillow. "Now," he said. "I have my own little room."

She smiled and, pulling a blanket from the bed, handed it over to him. "I think we shall sleep much more soundly this way," she said.

"Agreed," he said, arranging his scant bed linens and sitting on the floor. "Good night, sweet princess."

"Good night," she said, as she climbed into the bed.

He stretched out on the floor and, putting his hands behind his head to stare at the ceiling, he wondered if he would sleep at all with her so close and the memory of her body pressed against him still imprinted on his skin.

CAMILLE CLOSED HER EYES AND REVELED IN THE FEEL OF Bradley's body against hers. She had never been hugged so closely by a man. The sensation was nothing that she had experienced before. And something she anticipated experiencing again as soon as possible. She replayed the entire interaction over and over in her head. How he'd kissed the top of her head and kissed the tear from her cheek.

His kisses evoked the sensation of being cherished and loved. Loved. The word echoed in her mind, then settled in her thoughts. She was falling in love with this man. This man from the future who knew so little about her world. This man who had nothing to his name. Her father would be appalled.

She smiled at the thought. Her father, who had tried so fervently to match her with a wealthy man of his circle, would not react favorably to his only daughter falling in love with this man who had no family pedigree and not even a means of support. His name was unknown to them, though he may be known in Natchez, since his sister lived there.

His sister.

Her eyes flew open and she had to catch her breath. Bradley's sister. In Natchez. It hadn't occurred to her before this moment that in order for Bradley's sister to be in Natchez, then she too must have travelled back in time. And probably his grandmother, too, but she would have to think about that later.

If Bradley's sister had travelled back in time, then how did she end up in Natchez? Camille had assumed that Bradley was from New Orleans, but now she needed more information. Was he traveling to Natchez in order to return to his own time?

No. She pressed her hands against her head to stop the oncoming headache. Bradley had traveled through time in New Orleans. She knew this for certain because she had been there.

She would never get any sleep if she allowed her thoughts to continue racing in this fashion.

I have to sleep. I'll sort this out in the morning.

She turned on her side and, even though it was too dark to see them, faced the trunks Bradley had placed between them. She wished he hadn't put them there, even though she understood he was only trying to protect her. She strained, but couldn't hear him breathing. She had liked it better when he snored ever so softly. Perhaps he wasn't asleep.

BRADLEY WASN'T SURE HOW LONG HE LAY WIDE AWAKE, BUT eventually he drifted into a light slumber.

Just as the first streaks of dawn began to break the darkness, he woke to a clamor, the likes of which he hadn't heard since the last time he went to a college football game. Camille was his first thought as he sat up. He peered through the pale light, but she appeared to be still asleep. He wondered how anyone could possibly sleep through the yelling and cheering coming from somewhere on the ship.

He got up and hesitated, trying to decide if he should wake her. Coming to the decision that he couldn't leave her here alone, he went to her bed and whispered her name. She stirred, but didn't open her eyes. She was so peaceful, her lashes smudged against her skin, her lips parted in a peaceful expression, turned up slightly at the corners. He regretted interrupting her good dreams.

Leaning over, he kissed her on the cheek and as he straightened, her eyes opened. Delighted, he smiled.

Her peaceful expression turned to one of alarm. "What's that noise?" she asked.

"I don't know. I think we should go find out."

"I agree," she said, throwing off the blanket and moving to the window to peer out through the breaking dawn. "It's a race," she said.

"A race?"

"A steamboat race. It happens all the time," she explained. "Two captains decide to see whose ship is faster."

Though her expression was dispassionate, her words struck fear in his heart. He'd read the accounts of the horrific steamboat explosions. Death by fire and water. "We have to get out of here," he said, taking her hand, and pulling her toward the door.

She went with him. Surely she'd heard of the explosions. He searched his memory, but couldn't remember if any happened before 1838, but he was almost certain they had. Either way, he wanted no part of it.

When they got out on the deck, it was more crowded than it had been. They could barely walk, there were so many people.

And worse, they were yelling and cheering. Bradley held onto her hand as he pulled her with him toward the railing.

There. He saw the other boat through the mist on the river. Fortunately, the two boats were far apart. "We have to get off of here," he said.

"And go where?" Camille asked, gesturing toward the river.

She was right. The Mississippi River was so wide, they may as well be on the ocean.

Or in the air. The realization stirred him to action.

He had to get to the captain. He had to get him to stop this insanity. "I have to get to the captain," he said, yelling so she could hear.

"It won't do any good," she said, gazing toward the bank.

"Are we going to miss our stop?"

"Probably."

How could she be so unaffected? She wiped at her eyes and yawned. She was still half asleep. He smiled in spite of himself and pulled her to him. It was easy to pull her to him in the crowd. No one noticed and it kept her safe. "I have to find the captain," he said into her ear. "If we don't slow down, the ship could explode."

"They do this all the time," she said. "It's kind of a good thing. It means we'll get to Natchez faster."

"We're gonna miss our stop," he said. *If we get there at all.*

"I'll wait here," she said, looking around for a place to sit.

"No way," he replied. "I'm not leaving you alone with all this going on." He pulled her by the hand toward the stairs leading up to the captain's deck.

"We can't go up there," she said, pulling back, her eyes wide open now.

He stood, one foot on the step leading up to the captain's area, and one foot on the deck with Camille. "All right," he agreed. "You stay right here. I'll be right back. Don't move. Okay?"

"Oh." She scowled. "All right."

It was the best he could do. He left her standing there and dashed up the rickety wooden stairs leading to the captain's area. As he neared the top, he heard the Captain yelling at the other steamboat captain.

"You'll never catch me, you sorry son of a gun! You're a worthless bucket of steam."

Bradley smelled the alcohol before he even got to the top step. The captain was swaying and yelling at the top of his lungs. He was a fully bearded fellow with a uniform that had clearly seen better days.

Bradley saw an overhead rope and two ropes leading down. "Sir," he said. "Captain?"

"Come on in and join the fun, my boy," the Captain said. "Captain John Crawford is my name."

"And my name is Captain Becquerel."

"You're a captain, too?" he asked, a moment of clarity passing through his eyes, then was gone. Bradley wondered if he imagined it.

"I am. And I'm here to help you." Bradley took a quick survey of the situation. It was a good thing he was mechanically inclined and he sent a silent thank you to his grandfather for dragging him through all those museums when he was growing up. "How long have you been awake?" Bradley asked, under the guise of making conversation while he assessed the situation.

"Oh, I've been awake since time began."

"Well, in that case, shouldn't you get a little sleep?"

"I don't need no shut eye boy. I can stay up as long as my ship can outrun that one over there. That damn Captain thinks he can outrun me. He's as daft as the day is long."

While the captain was intent on his rant, Bradley slowly pulled a lever that he hoped would decrease the pressure in the boilers down to a safe level.

The ship began to slow, but the uproar from below on the deck increased in protest.

"Do you have a co-pilot?" Bradley asked, attempting to keep the drunken captain distracted from losing the race.

"Tom? I sent that worthless young'un to bed hours ago. Now my boy is in the boiler room. Let's tell him to add some more fuel, shall we?" He pulled on the rope that led below.

It was probably for the best. Captain Crawford probably would have sucked Tom into his drunken insanity. The captain was sitting now. Ranting about the other captain, the Mississippi River, and a myriad of other nonsensical things, all the while waving his bottle of liquor.

Bradley knew absolutely nothing about piloting a steamboat, but nonetheless, he grabbed hold of the wheel and hoped he could keep it away from sandbars until the mysterious copilot named Tom showed up. In the meantime, while the captain was distracted, he pulled on the rope that set off the steam whistle which at the same time, decreased the pressure on the boilers. The boy in the engine room was doubtless confused by now, but the ship was slowing and that was all that mattered.

The noise from the crowd below decreased to a low grumbling as the ship slowed to a crawl. Captain Crawford had passed out

"Bradley!" Camille appeared at the door and saw him behind the wheel. "Where's the captain?"

"Unfortunately, Captain Crawford had a little too much."

Her gazed landed on the captain, passed out. Her lips twitched up at the corners for a fleeting moment, before she turned back to him, her voice urgent. "We're not far from Natchez," she said. "If we don't stop soon, we're gonna miss our stop."

Bradley turned and fiddled with the ropes some more, doing the opposite of what he'd seen the captain do. There was nothing he wanted right now than to get off this boat. "We've got to find Tom. Otherwise, there's no one to pilot this boat."

"I'll take care of it," she said and disappeared as quickly as she had come.

He saw her on the deck below, talking to a couple of men who subsequently scattered. She then gathered up her skirts, turned, and disappeared. A minute later, she reappeared at the door. "Someone is going to wake Tom and I sent for our trunks." She bit her lip as she studied the large wheel. "Can you get us a little closer to the bank?"

Bradley was already working on that. He saw bluffs up ahead on the right. "Is that it?" he asked.

"Yes. That's Natchez Under the Hill. We'll get transportation there and go up to the town. Then..." She locked her green eyes onto his. "Then we can find your sister. Do you know where she might be?"

He turned back to the ropes to avoid her gaze. He'd always pictured her at his grandparents' plantation, but she could easily have left there by now.

No. He reminded himself that her portrait had been painted and survived close to two hundred years at the house. She would be there. If she wasn't, they would know where to find her. "Yes," he said. "I know where to find her." He even knew the address, but doubted it had an address yet. It would be known as the Becquerel Plantation.

As they drifted toward the bank, the copilot entered the captain's area. Bleary-eyed from sleep, he took one glance at Captain Crawford and shook his head. "Thank you for being here," he said. "That bloody..." he glanced at Camille, "fellow will get us all killed one day."

"I'm happy I could be of assistance," Bradley said. "But mostly, I'm happy this is my stop."

"Your name, Sir?"

"Bradley Becquerel."

"Ah, the Becquerel name is well-known in these parts. Now you'll be one who saved the day."

"Please, no need for that," Bradley said, a flash of horror going through his mind at his name appearing in the history books and what implications that might spell for his future self. "I was in the right time at the right place."

"Very well," Tom said, shaking Bradley's hand while he kept another on the wheel. "If you ever need a job, let me know and I'll be more than happy to make sure you're hired."

A little light bulb went off in Bradley's mind and he glanced at Camille. "I may take you up on that," he said. A steamboat pilot. A worthy career that he hadn't even thought to consider. He tucked it into the back of his mind as he helped Camille down the narrows stairs to the common deck area and they located their trunks which had been brought up from their cabin.

They got into the small yawl boat and Bradley experienced an intense sense of relief at being off the riverboat coupled with anticipation at seeing his sister again. As they neared land, he was in awe at the sight of Natchez Under the Hill. In his time, it was nothing more than a slice of history visited by the occasional tourist. But here, in this day, Natchez Under the Hill was a small town in itself. It was crowded with wagons full of freight and people on horseback, some apparently just there to see the steamboat.

Once they were on land, they secured a horse and wagon - what appeared to be their version of taxi. Riding in the wagon along the road leading away from the dock, he stared at the booming town.

There was a row of buildings, eating establishments, stores, and what appeared to gentlemen's clubs if the ladies watching them from the balconies was any indication. He caught himself staring, but got himself in check before getting no more than a raised eyebrow from Camille.

He grinned sheepishly. "It's much different now," he said. By standards of the future, the ladies were more than overdressed.

As the smell of food drifted through the air, Bradley's stomach growled. "Should we get something to eat for breakfast?"

Camille scowled at him. Then laughed. "You've never been here before."

"Sort of, but not really," he said. "I remember it much differently."

"Well, you might enjoy eating here, Under the Hill, but I don't think you want me to be with you."

"Why not?" He asked, "It smells really good. And I'm starved."

She leaned over and whispered in his ear. "It's a place of ill-repute."

"Ah," he said, as understanding dawned. He remembered stories his grandfather had told him, but being here and seeing it was an entirely different thing.

"Where are we headed?" the driver called back over his shoulder.

Camille looked expectantly at Bradley. Oddly enough, this was more his territory now than hers. The sensation was a bit disturbing. "Becquerel Plantation," he said, with all the confidence he could muster given the situation.

"I'll have you there in two shakes of a lamb's tale," the driver said and they rode through town and up the hill to the more reputable part of Natchez.

Bradley marveled at how different everything looked. The unpaved streets. The people on horseback and on foot – all dressed in what looked like formal clothing. The wooden storefronts as they passed through downtown. The white church that still stood to this day.

"We can get something to eat here if you want to," Camille said as they passed a café.

"Do you want to stop, Miss?" the driver asked.

They agreed to stop and went into a restaurant with white table cloths. Bradley wondered if this was the same building where he had lunch with his grandfather what now seemed like an eternity ago.

"This seems familiar to you," Camille observed.

"A little bit," he said. "I suppose small towns don't change as much as cities."

"But Natchez is a city," she said, glancing toward the window where people moved to and fro, her expression perplexed.

He smiled. "You're right. It is."

Her eyes narrowed. "It is now, but it won't be."

The waitress came to their table and they ordered eggs, cornbread, dried apples, coffee for Bradley and cold tea for Camille.

The waitress suggested flapjacks and molasses, so they added that to their order.

As they waited for their food, for the first time since last night, Bradley had the time to just gaze into Camille's eyes.

She was wearing the same clothes she had worn when they set out on this trip and he suspected that she rarely allowed that to happen.

"It'll be nice," he said, "to freshen up and change clothes."

She agreed whole-heartedly. "We brought all those clothes and haven't had the opportunity to change."

"And even after we managed to get a cabin," he agreed.

"If it hadn't been for that daft riverboat captain."

Bradley grew serious. "He endangered our lives. I know I stepped over a boundary with that, but someone had to do something."

"I was very impressed," she said.

"Then it was worth it," he said, the smile back on his lips. "And, who knows, I may have found work."

"Maybe," she agreed, lowering her gaze. Before he could ask her about her less than enthusiastic response, their food arrived. He decided to let it go. It wasn't important anyway.

"It's going to rain," Camille remarked off-handedly.

Bradley glanced out the window at the bright sunshine. He knew better than to question her though. He learned quickly.

After they finished their breakfast, Camille reached into her pocket and handed him some coins. "For you to pay with," she whispered.

Bradley paid a man who came around to the tables. He would have to ask her later about females not handling money.

However, once they were back in the buggy, he was reminded that the driver could hear their conversation, so he again, decided not to bring it up.

The driver turned south and headed down what would probably be a highway someday.

They turned down an even less traveled road and Bradley began to recognize landmarks. Not buildings, but the terrain. Then he recognized a house that belonged to his grandfather's neighbor.

Bradley began to feel fidgety. He felt like he needed to walk or perhaps even get out of the buggy and run, though he certainly wouldn't get there any faster.

He had the sensation that he was going home. He knew that his grandfather wouldn't be there, but he couldn't shake the feeling that he would be.

Perhaps it was the weather. There was an electricity in the air. Not only was it going to rain, it was going to storm. The dark cloud was to the east and the wind was picking up.

Whatever it was, the weather or the anticipation, Bradley wanted to be there already. He'd never been on such on interminable long trip.

"Are you alright?" she asked as they turned down an oak lined lane. "You must be nervous about being here."

He glanced at her, unable to keep his gaze focused on any one thing – even her at the moment. He nodded and she sat quietly next to him.

They rounded the curve and he could see the house up ahead. His drew in his breath sharply. And nearly came out of his skin. It was the same. His head spun a little at the impossibility of being here at his grandfather's house. In 1838.

Camille reached out and put her hand over his. He felt her support through that simple touch.

"Thank you," he said, looking into her green eyes before his gaze bounced back to the house.

"We just made it before the rain," the driver said. "I'd have to stop and put the cover up if we had much further to go."

Even as the driver said that, a raindrop landed on Bradley's forehead.

As they pulled into the circle drive, Camille handed him some more coins. Bradley took the money, but didn't bother counting it or worrying about if it was an appropriate amount to pay. He just handed the money to the driver and after getting down himself, helped Camille from the buggy. It was imperative that they get to the porch before the rain set in.

Taking her hand, they raced to the steps leading to the porch. Laughing as they raced to beat the rain, raindrops started falling. Breathless, they gathered under the porch. "You need that umbrella of yours," she pointed out.

"Where is my umbrella?" he asked.

"I think my father has it," she said. "He's trying to find out where you bought it so he can get one like it."

"I'm glad he didn't ask me," he said, wondering how he would explain having an umbrella from Target.

He watched as the driver brought their trunks to the porch. Perhaps the driver should wait for them in case Erika wasn't here.

Perhaps they should have spent the night in Natchez so they could clean up before coming to visit.

He took a deep breath. Now was not the time for anxiety.

Camille looked at him questioningly. "Ready?" she asked.

"I'm not sure," he said. Then, going on impulse, he held out his hand and drew her toward him. "Thank you," he murmured, his cheek against hers. "Thank you for coming with me."

She didn't answer. She just put her arms around him and held him close. When he released her, she said. "Come on, let's find Erika."

He followed her to the door and lifted the heavy iron door knocker. Dropped it against the door.

Within minutes, a tall black man dressed all in black, appeared at the door. "How may I assist you?" he asked.

In the seconds Bradley was trying to decide the best way to ask for his sister, Camille said, "We've come to call on Miss Erika Becquerel."

A perplexed expression crossed the man's features, then he stepped back to allow them to enter.

"Who may I tell her is calling?" he asked.

"Bradley," he said, his heart doing a funny little flip. She must be here.

The butler closed the door behind them.

The first thing Bradley saw when he stepped inside was the grandfather clock standing in the foyer. The same exact clock that stood in that very same spot today. In the future.

"You may wait in the parlor," the butler said, nodding toward their right, and went upstairs.

Bradley stood transfixed in front of the clock.

"Bradley?"

The rain was heavy now and thunder rumbled overhead. The house smelled... different. He found it odd that that was the only thing that seemed significantly different. That and perhaps the quietness. There was no hum of air conditioning or anything electrical. Except for the ticking of the clock, the house was quiet.

"Bradley," Camille said, taking his hand and tugging him gently toward the room on the right.

The clock began chiming the hour and he was drawn back to stand in front of the clock. He counted eleven chimes. Eleven o'clock. The chiming still echoing in his mind along with a rumble of thunder, his attention was drawn to the top of the staircase on the landing. Lightening flashed through the window at the top of the landing. His hand slipped from hers and he moved to stand in front of the stairway.

A lovely woman in a long green dress with her hair swept to one side stood on the landing. Her skirt gathered in her hands, she appeared poised to continue down the stairs. However, when their eyes met, she froze.

Recognition dawned.

It was Erika.

He saw the moment his sister recognized him. He took a step forward, a lump in his throat.

She was here. She was actually here. Alive.

Tears welled in his eyes. He couldn't move.

"Bradley!" Erika said, lowering a foot on the stairs as she put a hand on the banister.

Thunder crashed through the house as he put a foot on the bottom step.

"Erika," he said, his heart swelling with joy.

Then something happened.

He blinked and she was gone.

CHAPTER 10

"No!" Camille gasped and rushed forward.

It had happened again. Only this time, it was much quicker.

Before, in New Orleans, he had seemed to fade.

But here, this time, he had just... vanished.

The woman at the top of the stairs, rushed down and stood in the spot where he had been.

"No!" Erika said, echoing Camille's denial. She looked around them frantically, turning in a circle, her skirts twirling around her.

"He was here," she said, looking to Camille as though for confirmation.

Camille swallowed the thickness in her throat "Yes," she said.

They'd travelled all this way to find Erika and now Bradley vanished in an instant.

"It was Bradley," she said, pinning her gaze on Camille.

Camille nodded. "You're his sister."

"Yes." Erika said. She stopped and took Camille's arms. "My brother was here. Just a moment ago."

Camille nodded.

"How did he get here?"

"We came by steamboat from New Orleans."

"We. Who are you? Are you…?

"I'm Camille Lafleur," Camille felt her chin go up a notch.

"You're Bradley's friend."

Friend. The word didn't seem to accurately describe her relationship with Bradley. Yes, they were friends, but there was more than that. He was more than that to her her. "Yes," she said.

"You don't seem surprised that he… vanished."

A little surprised, but more acutely disappointed. And worried. "I've seen it happen before."

"Are you from…" Erika glanced around, lowered her voice. "From now?"

Camille smiled. She suddenly understood what Erika was asking. She wanted to know if Camille had come from the future with Bradley or if he had met her here in this time. "Yes. Bradley is from the future."

Erika laughed a watery laugh. "Yes, he's from the future. But where did he go?"

"Back?"

"Why would he do that?" she asked, to no one in particular, twirling again, to face the grandfather clock. She studied its face as though if could offer an answer.

"He'll return," Camille said. *If he can.*

"Oh my God," Erika said. "I never thought to see him again." She went to sit on the bottom step of the stairs and rubbed her hands over her face. "This is so… unexpected."

Camille went to sit next to her. "He was so excited to see you. We spent days traveling from New Orleans. He suffered from nerves about it, too."

"Nerves. Why would he be nervous?" She asked, turning to face Camille.

"He wasn't really sure you would be here."

"I guess not," she said. "It must have been hard for him."

"It was hard for him. I think he missed you very much."

Her words brought tears to Erika's eyes.

"I'm sorry," Camille said. "I don't mean to make you sad. He was so very excited to see you."

Erika wiped at her eyes. "It's okay. I just never thought I'd see him again. Not even for an instant."

"Oh," Camille repeated. "Okay. I heard Bradley say that word."

Erika's eyes widened. "It's a common expression in… in."

"In the future," Camille finished for her. Then attempted a bright smile.

"I wonder," Erika said, shaking her head. "As far as you know, he came back while in New Orleans?"

"I'm certain of that. Like I said, I was there."

"I always thought it was this house."

"It must be this house," Camille said, "since he barely got inside the door."

"Why New Orleans?" Erika asked, seemingly to herself, staring into space. "What's there? He never liked New Orleans."

Camille wasn't sure what to say. Did she tell Bradley's sister that the two of them had a… connection?

Now that the question was posed, Camille realized she had assumed she was what drew him back in time.

Erika pinned her gaze onto Camille's. "You," she said. "He'd drawn to you."

Camille wasn't sure how to respond. She wanted it to be true. She wanted Bradley to be drawn to her. She wanted him to come back. To her. "I don't know," she murmured, tearing her gaze away.

"Erika?" A man's voice called from the top of the stairs. Camille turned to see a tall, handsome man with dark hair standing on the landing. She watched as he came down the stairs. The girls moved their skirts aside for him to pass. He stood next to Erika, with his hand on her shoulder, smiling down at her. She tipped her chin up and smiled back at him. The love between them was evident in that one exchange.

"Charles," she said, "I'd like to introduce you to Miss Camille Lafleur. Camille, this is my husband, Charles Becquerel."

"The pleasure is all mine," he said, holding his hand out for her.

She placed her hand in his, palm down, and his breathe grazed the back of her hand. His lips didn't touch her. "It's a pleasure to meet you, sir," she said.

"Camille is a friend of my brother's," Erika said, "up from New Orleans."

Something nagged at the back of Camille's mind as she was introduced to Erika's husband, but she too distracted to focus on it.

Charles's expression in response to this information went rapidly from neutral, to questioning, to incredulousness. "Your brother?" he echoed.

"Yes," Erika said, exuding a calmness that Camille was certain she couldn't possibly feel. "We're becoming acquainted."

Charles studied her curiously. "Is she from here?" he asked.

"Yes," Erika said. "From New Orleans."

"And your brother."

"He was here," she said, "but he had to return suddenly. Unexpectedly."

"That's unfortunate," he said, "I should very much like to meet your brother."

Erika nodded, the pain crossing her features again before she took her husband's hand in hers. "I didn't have the opportunity to speak to him before he... left."

"But he was here?" he asked.

"Yes."

"I thought he lived too far away to visit," Charles said. "This is indeed fortunate information."

Erika took a deep breath, turning back to Camille. "It's unexpected," she said.

"I'm on my way to the stables," he said. "I'll let you two visit."

She tilted her chin up again and he kissed her on the lips. A lock of dark hair fell across his forehead and Erika threaded her fingers in his dark hair, pulling him closer. Camille looked away, feeling as though she had intruded upon a private moment.

Charles left and Erika turned back to her, a satisfied smile on her face.

"I'm sorry to intrude," Camille said.

"Don't be silly." Erika laughed. "I should show you to the guest room," she said. "You must be exhausted after your long trip." She stood up. "I'll have a bath sent up."

Camille almost groaned. A bath! "That would be heavenly," she said.

"Villars will bring your trunks up. You may be here for awhile."

Camille felt a stab shoot through her heart. She was supposed to be back in New Orleans before her father returned. She couldn't stay here more than a week in order to do that. But she couldn't tell Erika that now. She had to think. And rest.

Within the hour, Camille was settled into the guest room and luxuriated in a steaming bubble bath. Though she'd been offered the assistance of a servant, she had declined.

She was alone at last. Alone to rest. And to let her mind wander.

She missed Bradley already. In a way, she wished she'd been holding his hand when he disappeared. Would she have gone with him? The thought of seeing the future sent goose bumps over her skin. He'd told her very little, but he'd implied enough for her to get the impression that the future was nothing like the present.

She couldn't even fathom what it must be like. But this house still stood. After all those years, his family's home still stood. So, the world had not completely changed.

She washed her hair, then stayed in the bath until the water cooled. The servant had brought up her trunks as Erika had promised and she looked forward to putting on a clean gown.

She didn't know how long she was expected to stay here. She could send her father a note. And let him know that she would be delayed.

From a trip she hadn't told him about.

Her father would be irate. Camille would probably never be allowed to work in the tavern again. Her father would probably ban her to the plantation forever.

Or marry her off to some elderly widower.

The thought sent a stab of horror through her. She would be considered ruined after running off with a man. It didn't matter that nothing had happened. She would have to be married quickly before the scandal took root and completely ruined her reputation.

She ducked her head under the water to rinse her hair. This was not good.

This was a disaster.

Perhaps she just needed to stay here. At least until her father's ire lessened. He would never understand.

Camille stepped out of the bath and dried off. She chose a simple green day dress from her trunk and pulled it on over her head. She put on her stockings and shoes. She then went to the window and looked out over the empty fields. It was early spring, so the cotton planting hadn't begun yet.

She realized she was stalling. Not knowing what to expect.

Taking a deep steadying breath, she went to the door and turned the doorknob.

The tall servant Villars was waiting on the other side. Camille jumped.

"Mistress Erika would like you to join her on the veranda," he said, leading the way, assuming she would follow.

Camille smiled to herself at his assumption that she would follow. He was right of course.

He led her down the stairs and out back to the veranda, then left her. Erika sat next to a small table with a pitcher of water next to her. She didn't see Camille at first. Her expression was sad. Anxious.

Camille watched her a moment, wondering what she must be thinking. Seeing her brother suddenly like this must be quite a shock. A brother she had never thought to see again.

And then to be cheated by only seeing him for a fleeting moment. It seemed cruel indeed.

When Erika sensed her standing there, she turned, her expression immediately changing to a smile, "Come," she said. "Sit and have some fresh water with strawberries. It's very refreshing."

Camille went to sit in next to Erika in the offered chair. She returned Erika's smile. She could definitely see the resemblance in their features. There was a mysteriousness about them. As though they knew things that others didn't. And indeed they did. They knew the future.

"It's very lovely here," Camille said.

"It's beautiful," Erika said.

"You must be quite content," Camille said, knowing she teetered on the boundary of prying. Erika, however, didn't seem to notice or maybe she didn't mind. Camille, after all, knew what she knew. Camille wondered how many others knew. Did Erika carry her burden alone. Or did her husband know.

"I am very content. I have a loving husband," she said and the love she felt for Charles in return showed in her eyes as she spoke of him. "There is no where I'd rather be."

"You had a choice then," Camille said.

"Yes," Erika admitted. "Eventually. Not so much at first."

"I wonder if Bradley has a choice," Camille wondered out loud as she watched a butterfly flitter around some pretty white flowers growing in a pot on the porch.

"I wonder, too," Erika said, her eyes glazing with unshed tears. She took a sip of water and seemed to steady herself.

"Tell me how you came to know him."

Camille told Erika everything. Well, almost everything. She left out the part about how much she wanted to kiss him. It didn't seem like an appropriate thing to discuss with anyone, much less the man's sister.

"Do you love him?" Erika asked.

Camille's eyes widened and her thoughts froze. So much for having what she considered an appropriate conversation with Bradley's sister.

Did she? Did she love him?

Her heart tripped when she saw him. She wanted to kiss him more than anything.

She missed him horribly.

She wanted him next to her.

She had traveled with him without even telling her family.

Did she love him?

"Yes," she breathed.

Erika inhaled sharply. "There's something we have to do," she said. "We have to see Vaughn."

CHAPTER 11

*B*radley stood staring at the silently ticking grandfather clock.

At the battle scar in the form of a jagged rip between the Roman numerals six and seven across its face that happened during the Civil War.

He noticed the soft hum of cool air coming from a vent in the ceiling. And the familiar music of the Weather Channel playing softly from a television in the kitchen.

His blood ran cold and his thoughts froze.

He was home.

He squeezed his eyes tightly closed and held onto the image of his sister standing at the top of the landing. She'd called out to him. She had been real.

What cruel twist of fate had allowed him to travel all the way from New Orleans to Natchez on a steamboat in 1838, risking his very life in the process, only to be whisked away in a heartbeat back to his own time?

It had been real? Hadn't it?

He ran his hands down his wool pants and studied the boots that were definitely from the past.

Camille had been standing next to him. He took comfort that she was with his sister. Erika would take care of her.

Only he hadn't had the opportunity to tell Erika how much Camille meant to him. Would

Camille tell her?

It occurred to him that Camille didn't know. How could she know when he hadn't bothered to tell her?

He had to tell her. He had to get back to her. His thoughts were tangled and he couldn't make sense of them.

He legs felt like rubber and he suddenly had no strength. He took a few steps and collapsed onto the bottom stair. Imagined Camille and Erika sitting here – talking. They wouldn't know what had happened to him.

Or would they?

They certainly wouldn't know why.

He didn't know why.

His thoughts racing jumbled through his mind, he looked up and saw his grandfather standing there.

Jonathan stared at him – incredulousness on his face. He looked as though he'd seen a ghost.

Bradley laughed. Was it out loud? Perhaps he was a ghost. He had no energy. No strength in his legs.

"Bradley?" his grandfather whispered.

"Grandpa?" Bradley answered, hope surging through him. Perhaps he was still alive.

Then Jonathan was next to him. "What happened Bradley? Are you alright?"

Bradley gazed into his grandfather's kind face. "I don't know. I was there. I was right there. And then I was here."

"How? No. Nevermind. Let's get you cleaned up and rested. Then you can tell me everything."

Bradley's first instinct was to resist. He needed to get back to Camille. To Erika. But Jonathan was right. He need to clean up and rest. To sort things through. To figure out what he needed to do next.

THE NEXT DAY, BRADLEY WAS IN HIS GRANDFATHER'S WHITE Lexus sedan driving from Natchez to New Orleans. What torture was this? First he had to endure the steamboat trip. Now a trip in the car. What good was being a pilot when he had no way to fly?

He'd called the hotel and they said they had his things in the front office. There was nothing of value, really, except the money. But he hadn't had the courage to ask about it. He knew the odds of it being there were slim. He never carried over a hundred dollars in his money clip. It could disappear too easily. He used credit cards so a stolen card could easily be cancelled and fraudulent charges reversed.

But not in 1838.

His nerves on edge, he parked and hurried to the front desk, knowing it would do no good to hurry. If his money was stolen, there was nothing he could do about it at this point.

"I'm Bradley Becquerel. You have things from my room."

He didn't recognize the girl behind the counter. "I'll check," she said. A couple of minutes later she rolled his suitcase around the counter and parked it at his feet. "You need to check out." She said.

"You have my credit card for the nights I was here," he said.

"Right, but you never checked out, so we extended your stay."

"What? You went into my room and gathered up my thing. You knew I wasn't here," he said.

"Let me check," she said again and disappeared to the back.

Bradley tapped his fingertips on the counter, forcing himself to not open his suitcase right there in the lobby.

A few minutes later, the manager followed her out. "Hey, man," he said. "I'm glad to see you're alive."

"I haven't been here in a week," Bradley said, tapping his suitcase. "It looks like housekeeping brought my stuff down. I just need to pay for the nights I was here and be on my way."

The man tapped on the computer. "We checked you out yesterday after you called."

"But I wasn't here. I haven't been here since the night of the storm."

"Where were you then?"

"I was with a friend."

"Hey, man. It's New Orleans. People decide to stay and drink all the time. We don't force people out. We just extend the stay."

"But I wasn't here," he said. "You can't charge me for nights I wasn't here."

"Hey, if you're off drunk and hooked up somewhere, we don't kick you out of the room. We just extend the stay."

"You've got to be kidding." Bradley realized he was not going to win this argument. "Just charge it my credit card," he said.

"It's already done," the manager said. "Tell you what, I'll waive the fee for an unauthorized extended stay. Just plan on telling us next time."

"There won't be a next time," Bradley muttered to himself as he took the printout of the exorbitant charges to his credit card.

It doesn't matter, he told himself. *I just need to see if my money is in the suitcase.* Looking at the charges, he stopped as he walked toward the door. Deciding since they'd charged him so much, they needed to hear about it if anything was missing. He hefted his suitcase on a counter and went through it. His faded money was stuffed in there as well as the sack of coins. He didn't bother counting them. He wasn't sure how much he'd started with anyway.

Satisfied that he had what he came for, despite being severely overcharged for the room, he tossed the suitcase in the trunk of his grandfather's car and headed north. He checked the clock. He should be back by Midnight.

What he wouldn't give for an airplane right now, but it was oh so very much better than the steamboat.

Bradley had been traveling east about thirty minutes on Interstate ten when he heard a ringing sound that sounded vaguely familiar.

He laughed aloud as he realized he had discovered a cure for cell phone addiction – time-travel. He pulled over on the side of the road and opened the trunk. After rummaging around in his suitcase, he found his cell phone. Fortunately, he had left it charging and since housekeeping had unplugged it only yesterday, it still had a full charge.

As he got back into the driver's seat, his friend Mark' face popped up on the screen. "Hello," he said.

"Bradley, is that you?"

"Of course.

"Where the hell have you been?"

"I was out of pocket," Bradley said, saying the first thing that came to his mind.

"There's a girl," Mark said.

"You got me," Bradley said, allowing Mark to make assumptions that required little or no explanation, unlike the truth.

"That explains it. I've been trying to reach you."

"What' up?"

"We have a meeting in Ft. Worth today at 5:00 with Noah Worthington of Skye Travel." When Bradley didn't immediately respond, Mark continued. "THE Noah Worthington."

"I know who he is."

"You have to be there. We've been trying to get an interview with him since we were in college."

"I'm driving."

"Where are you? I'll come pick you up."

"I'm just east of New Orleans on Interstate ten."

"I'll pick you up at Ryan Field."

The Baton Rouge airport was on his way. "I'm supposed to be at my grandfather's house in Natchez tonight," he said.

"Call him. Tell him you'll be there tomorrow. He'll understand. Why are you driving anyway?"

"It's a long story."

"This is a life changing interview," Mark said. "You have to be there. It's a once in a lifetime opportunity."

Mark was right. Working for Noah Worthington would be better than even working for a major airline. More control over his schedule and destinations. Well, maybe not at first, but eventually. And even more money. His friend's words began to sink in. This had been his goal from the outset. Since before he'd even earned his pilot's license.

"Okay," Bradley said. "Pick me up at BTR."

CAMILLE AND ERIKA WALKED DOWN THE STAIRS AND ALONG A shaded path away from the house. It was the opposite direction from the cotton fields and the servants' houses.

Erika explained that this was the way to the guest house and as well as the garçonnière. When they passed by the bachelor's quarters, Camille giggled.

"What's funny?" Erika asked.

"I was just remembering my brother's garçonnière. We had so much fun there!"

"At your brother's garçonnière? I thought the whole point was to keep the boys away from their sisters."

"Ah," Camille said. "That's hog wash. We were so excited when my father moved them out to their apartment."

"Your mother let you go?"

"Oh course. I spent all my time with my brothers anyway. When we weren't studying, of course. Or practicing the piano." She wrinkled her nose.

"I take it you weren't a big fan of piano."

"Not at all. Horses were much more exciting," Camille said offhand, as they turned and walked along another path. "Why does Vaughn live so far away from the main house?"

"It's a rather long story, I'm afraid," Erika said.

As they approached the house with its little picket fence, a little shiver ran down Camille's spine. She was reminded of Madame Laveau. She'd said there was a woman in Natchez who could travel through time. Camille shivered as the words came back to her. *The woman is able to move freely about through time. The spell, some say, passed to her grandchildren.*

As Erika raised a hand to knock on the door, it swung open and an elegant older woman beckoned them inside. She drew Erika into a hug, then invited them into her parlor.

"Grandmother," Erika said, "I'd like you to meet Camille."

Camille thoughts froze. Grandmother. Vaughn. The illustrious Vaughn was Erika's grandmother? That meant Vaughn was also Bradley's grandmother. Oh. My. Madame Laveau had been right.

"It's lovely to meet you Camille," Vaughn said, her expression serene. "Please, sit on the sofa."

Camille sat on the sofa, while Erika and Vaughn each sat on chairs.

Erika sat on the edge of her chair and appeared to be about to burst with her news. "Grandmother," she said. "Camille is Bradley's friend."

Vaughn's face paled. Seconds passed.

Vaughn's expression shifted to one of concern. "Bradley," she whispered.

She shifted to sit on the sofa next to Camille and took her hands in hers. Vaughn had bright green eyes. Eyes that seemed to peer into Camille's very soul. "How do you know my grandson?" she asked, her hands squeezing Camille's.

Camille glanced questioningly at Erika. Erika nodded. "Tell her," she implored.

"Bradley came into my tavern. In New Orleans."

"What year?" Vaughn interrupted, urgency in her tone.

"This one," Camille said.

"Go on."

"I thought," she swallowed. The intensity emanating from the two women was almost overwhelming. "I thought he was a ghost at first because he disappeared. But then Madame Laveau said he couldn't possibly be a ghost because I knew he had blue eyes." Now that she'd started, she wanted to tell them everything.

"He didn't come back for awhile and I thought he was gone for good, but then he was back. Madame Laveau said he should come to see you. And Bradley wanted to see Erika. He didn't know you were here. He thinks you're... Anyway, so I came with him. My father doesn't know. He'll be furious if he finds out."

"Where is he?" Vaughn turned to Erika.

"He was here, but I only saw him for a few seconds before he was gone."

"You're certain it was him?" Vaughn asked.

"Absolutely," Erika said.

"He disappeared?"

Erika and Camille both nodded. "He was only inside the front door for a few minutes," Erika said.

"The butler asked us to wait while he went to get Erika," Camille said.

"But as soon as I spoke to him," Erika said. "he was gone."

Vaughn pulled away, holding her hands together in her lap. She stared straight ahead in silence as the seconds ticked past.

"It was too much," she said, turning to Erika. "Seeing you was too much for him."

Erika looked like she was going to cry. "It's my fault."

"No," Vaughn said. "I must think. Go. Leave me. I'll summon you in due time."

CHAPTER 12

*N*oah Worthington was legendary in the flying world. Bradley was pleasantly surprised that he lived up to that image in real life.

But Bradley couldn't help but believe that he owed a huge chunk of his success to his wife Savannah. He'd even named his company after her. Her maiden name was Savannah Skye Richards. His company was Skye Travels. The honor was well-deserved. She had a smile that lit up the room and a kindness that made everyone feel welcome.

They met in Ft. Worth at the Saint Emilion restaurant and were instantly ensconced in an upscale cozy atmosphere.

Noah and Savannah sat at a table, their heads bent in conversation. The host took their names and after consulting with Noah, led them over to his table. Noah stood as introductions were made.

"Was your flight uneventful?" Noah asked.

"It was quite pleasant, actually," Mark said.

After they settled in, Savannah sipped her wine and turned her attention on Bradley. "How long have you two known each other?"

"We met in school," Mark said.

Savannah kept her eyes on Bradley. "You fly together often?"

"Not lately," Bradley said, "but in college we flew together a good bit," he said, glancing at Mark. Mark was obviously struggling with letting Bradley take the conversation.

"Why Skye Travel?" she asked.

Did she have to ask? Bradley glanced at Mark, but Mark just shrugged. It was apparent that Savannah was focused on Bradley. "Skye Travel is legendary. Even before I sat in the cockpit, I knew I wanted to fly for Skye."

She tilted her head, smiled, and waited for him to continue.

Bradley shifted his feet, then caught himself. It was valid question. "You treat your people like family," he said. "At least that's what everyone says. And you take the time and effort to mentor. Working for Skye Travels is more like an apprenticeship than a job. An apprenticeship that pays. Not to mention the opportunity to invest in the company. Some say you're thinking about starting to franchise."

Noah grinned at him. "I couldn't have said it better myself."

Bradley took a deep breath. He felt a flash of guilt. Mark had been the one to set this meeting up. And here Bradley was stealing the show. He'd been under the impression that they would be hired as a team.

When Savannah turned her attention on his friend, he released a silent sigh of relief.

"Mark, tell us about the most dangerous thing you ever did in an airplane."

Mark blanched. Nonetheless, he was quick on his feet. "I never take chances in the air. There are no old pilots with stories of daredevil chances."

Bradley eyed his friend quizzically. He knew Mark was lying. He knew there had been a low pass last month. Could Noah possibly know about that? Of course, he could. Noah knew everything about the pilots he interviewed.

"Is that something you've decided through experience or something you were taught in the classroom?" Noah asked.

Bradley was thankful that hadn't been his question. He couldn't think of a good answer. Mark was dead-meat no matter which answer he gave. Noah, he decided, definitely knew about the low pass.

Mark fumbled his way through that question and a few others. Bradley hated seeing his friend squirm. Mark had been more excited about the interview than Bradley. Until this moment Bradley had been ready to ditch life as he knew it and travel back in time to be with Camille.

Watching Savannah and Noah together brought back memories of Camille and their own easy relationship. A relationship like that could only come naturally. He knew that relationships took work, but there had to be something to build on.

Realizing someone had called his name, he blinked and saw that all three of them were watching him. "I was just wondering how you manage to do it all." He grinned at Savannah.

She laughed. "It's not easy. Not with a toddler at home, a company based out of Ft. Worth, and studying."

Three hours later, Noah and Mark had agreed on terms and had agreed to meet at Noah's office downtown the next morning. Bradley wasn't sure, but he had a feeling he'd carried Mark through the interview. A low pass could be a career breaker. Mark had gotten a lucky break.

Noah had insisted they stay the night at a nearby hotel, so for the first time since Mark had picked him up in Baton Rouge, Bradley had time to think about something other than flying.

Camille.

He pressed his fingers against the bridge of his nose. He was still in awe that he had seen his sister, even if only for a brief moment in time. He now had an image of her alive and well instead of thinking of her as dead.

Tomorrow he would take the job. He had to. Everything he'd worked for up to this point led to this job with Skye Travels.

If he couldn't get back in time, he couldn't just be homeless. He had to have a job. He leaned against the window sill and watched the cars, no more than Matchbox toys from this distance, and contemplated how much the country had changed.

He laughed at himself. Most would want to put him in an insane asylum. He was a successful pilot with a bright future. A man whose thoughts were focused on two centuries in the past. And a woman who lived there.

A police car, its bright lights flashing and the muted sounds of its sirens blaring caught his attention below. He felt far away as though watching something that wasn't real, amplifying his feeling of being disconnected from modern life.

A text came in from Mark. *Are you coming down to the bar for a drink to celebrate?*

Was Mark seriously going to drink the night before starting a new job with Noah Worthington? Bradley didn't have the energy to argue the point. *Flying tomorrow. Need to sleep.*

Leaving the window and the hustle and bustle of the modern world, he climbed into the bed and powered on his computer. He started by googling *Natchez 1830s.*

CAMILLE BENT AND PICKED A TINY BLUE WILDFLOWER AS SHE walked along a path away from the house. She chose the woodsy path over the fields. The air was warm. Only a few degrees more, and she'd have chosen to sit in the shade instead. The sky was a clear, spotless blue. There was no rain on the horizon.

She stood, twirling the daisy between her fingers and searching the sky. Her thoughts were on Bradley. She replayed the feel of his lips on her palm. On her cheek. Closed her eyes and imagined what his lips would feel like on hers.

An unfamiliar roar filled her ears and her eyes flew open. The roar disappeared. Perhaps she had imagined it. She searched the sky. Searched for... something, but she didn't know what.

Since his sudden disappearance, she watched for Bradley. She expected him to be standing there at any turn.

She shook her head. Watching the sky for him had no logic. It wasn't like he was going to fly in like an eagle.

She walked a few steps, then stopped and closed her eyes again. But this time she only heard the soft twittering of birds in the old oak tree.

Erika had been more than kind and welcoming to her. She'd wanted to know everything about her brother and she'd told Camille some things about Bradley. Like how one of his favorite toys as a child was a red and blue kite. He'd spent hours keeping it in the air. Erika told her that Bradley had become quite proficient at flying his kite. So much so, that by the time he was fifteen, he had a collection of about ten kites. After that, he'd taken up other games that Erika merely described as *things boys liked to do.*

Camille had only seen a kite once. One of the neighbor's boys had one, but when her brothers visited other boys Camille didn't go. The boy had brought it over and her brothers had gone crazy for it. Camille smiled at the memory. Boys were so easily entertained. Perhaps it was Bradley's love of kites that had her thinking of him when looking skyward.

To be truthful, though, he was in her mind all the time. Her thoughts were full of him.

Camille couldn't stay here. There was a strong likelihood that Bradley would never return here. If it hadn't been for his sister, Erika, she would have begun again to believe that he was an angel. People didn't just disappear like that. No one else traveled through time. It truly was preposterous to even think such a thing was possible.

She sat on a low-hanging branch of a huge oak tree and studied the little miniature daisy in her hand. Nature itself was a miracle. No one could explain life. No one could explain God. Yet Camille knew it existed. She believed.

Just like she believed that Bradley had traveled here from the future. Believed and knew it in her heart. Just as she knew that she was in love with him.

No other man had come close to coaxing her from her home. But she would have followed him anywhere.

Without him, though, this wasn't where she belonged.

She needed to go home.

Bradley had found her once. If it was meant to be, he'd find her again.

If not, she was prepared to live her life as a spinster. Despite what everyone said, it wasn't necessary for a woman to marry. She could choose to be single if she so chose.

And without Bradley, she would not settle for someone she didn't love.

CHAPTER 13

*B*radley lowered the wheels on the Challenger 350 jet and touched down at MLU – Monroe, Louisiana Airport. There was a long taxi ahead and a little bit of a wait before he could get out of the plane, but he didn't mind. He enjoyed having the time to think and wind down after the flight.

It had been one month since his meeting with Noah Worthington. He and Mark had gone on the books of Skye Travel two days later. Noah had suddenly lost one of his best pilots to United, so he had several flights booked and needed a pilot. Noah had a newborn baby at home with his new wife, so he was taking a leave from flying. That left him in desperate need of two pilots.

Bradley and Mark had unknowingly been on his short list for some time. But if they hadn't been available, Noah would have gone to the next person on the list. There was no shortage of pilots waiting to sign up with Skye Travel which branded itself on having the largest floating fleet in America. They had incorporated the American flag into their logo and it was proudly emblazoned on the tail of each plane.

In the month since he'd taken the job with Skye Travel, he

barely spoken to anyone in his family – not his grandfather or his mother. He'd driven his grandfather's car to Natchez and Mark had flown him from there home to Houston. He would soon be moving to Ft. Worth in order to be closer to Skye Travels.

As he taxied toward the airport apron, he thought about his father. Although his sister had reconnected with their father to a limited degree, Bradley hadn't spoken to him since the day he walked out on them, leaving his mother in tears. His mother found a job and Jonathan helped them out with money, but the emotional damage his father had done to his mother had been more than Bradley could forgive.

He checked the time. He was meeting his mother and her husband at the Mohawk Tavern in two hours. His mother had been happily remarried for five years. Bradley liked the guy and as long as he treated her alright, he was happy for her.

An hour later, he parked the car he'd borrowed from the airport in a parking space at the restaurant parking lot. Since he was early, he went straight to the bar and ordered a beer.

Sitting at the bar reminded him of Camille, as most things did these days.

He opened his iPad as he waited. Some would probably say Bradley had gone mad. He had read every single thing he could find on the Internet about the late 1830s, Louisiana and Natchez, specifically. He'd exhausted every resource he could find. Now his Kindle was filled with books he'd downloaded. He'd decided that books might have information that wasn't available online.

He had just added another book to his Kindle when his mother came up next to him and drew him into a hug. "It's so good to see you, Sweetie," she said.

Bradley hugged his mother back, absorbing the familiar smell of her perfume. She looked happy. Relaxed. "How are you, Mom?" he asked.

"I'm well," Anna said, pulling her husband, Allen forward. "I thought you might be early."

He shook hands with Allen before the two of them sat next to him.

"We can get a table when you're ready," he said.

"There's no wait," his mother said. "if you want to finish your beer." He heard the strain in her voice as she glanced at his beer.

He smiled, pushed the beer away, "It's just a prop," he said. "Let get something to eat. I'm starved."

Once they were seated at the table, they asked the waiter to bring oysters on the half shell as an appetizer.

"How's your new job?" Anna asked. "Is it everything you thought it would be?"

"It's great," he said, but even he could hear the lack of enthusiasm in his voice.

"Have you heard from your sister?" she asked.

Bradley glanced at Allen. Shook his head. He'd wanted to tell his mother, but he wanted to tell her in private. When he'd originally set up this dinner with her, he hadn't planned on her bringing her husband.

"Oh," Anna asked, her eyes brightening. "I meant to tell you. We just hired a new girl right out of college. She's single. I told her about you and although she said she wasn't interested in dating anyone, I think you should stop by and meet her."

Bradley shook his head. "I'm not interested, Mom."

Anna dug in her handbag and pulled out her cell phone. "I took her picture," she said as she scrolled through the images on her phone.

"Did she know it?" he asked, but remembered he had a picture of Camille that she didn't know about. He told himself that was different because Camille was from the past and didn't even know what a photo was.

"Well, no, I don't think so, but just look at her," Anna said, handing her phone to Bradley.

The girl in the photo was pretty. His mother was right about that. But the thought of meeting her – of talking to her - churned his stomach.

Their oysters arrived as Bradley handed the phone back to his mother. Bradley had suddenly lost his appetite. He let his mother and Allen have the oysters and he ordered another cold beer, ignoring the look on his mother's face.

All he could think about was Camille. Her smile. Her laugh. Her smooth skin and full lips. Her bright green eyes.

Camille was all he wanted. There had never been anyone else like her. And there never would be.

Bradley's heart was branded with her.

And as much as he fought it. As much as he tried to move forward, there was no denying it.

This past month, he'd gone about his business. He'd taken the new job – the job of his dreams. But his heart hadn't been in it. After work, he went home and isolated. He didn't talk to anyone he didn't have to.

His life was in the past.

"I can't go on like this," he said out loud.

"What?" his mother asked.

"I'm sorry, Mom," he said. "I can't do it. I can't meet anyone new."

"You have someone," she said.

He nodded. "I'm in love with a girl named Camille." As he said the words, his heart lightened, just a little. "If he could say it out loud, perhaps it was real.

"When do we get to meet her?"

Bradley scoffed.

The server took their food order and brought Bradley's beer. He needed to talk to his mother alone. There was no need to make Allen part of this. They had agreed at the beginning –

him, his mother, and Jonathan, to keep it between the three of them.

"We'll talk about it later," Bradley said. "Can I crash on your couch tonight?"

"No, but you can sleep in the guest room."

"It's finished?" he asked.

"New paint and new carpet," Allen said. "Your mother never runs out of projects for me to do."

Bradley would have to drop the car back at the airport and ride with his mother to their house. He couldn't keep the car overnight. It was going to be a long night and a lot of trouble, but he needed to get his mother alone. She was not going to be happy.

There was a strong possibility that she was about to lose her other child.

THE NEXT MORNING, AS BRADLEY WAITED TO TAXI DOWN THE runway, he absorbed the pages of a book that included journal entries written by a plantation mistress. Normally, before meeting Camille, he would have just flipped through the pages, looking for something that looked interesting.

But now that he had spent time in 1838 and had gotten to know the people and the customs, he read every word he could find. Every single word. It was as though he was afraid he would miss an important detail if he skipped over even a single line.

He had to put his iPad aside as he became airborne, but once he was in flight, he could monitor the plane and read, albeit a little more slowly.

As he monitored the controls and set the autopilot, his mind wandered back to his mother. There had been tears. He regretted that. But he felt he owed it to her to tell her what he was thinking instead of just disappearing. Just disappearing didn't seem fair to her. Especially since she no longer had her daughter either.

His mother was happy though in her life with Allen. It seemed that he deserved a chance at having happiness as well. Even if it brought his family pain.

The plane safely in route, he picked up his iPad and turned back to the book he was reading. He wasn't sure what he was looking for, but he knew he would know it when he saw it.

Deep in the world of 1838, one eye on the flight monitors, he froze. He'd found what he was looking for.

In 1839, a steamboat, The Orleans, had exploded on the way from Natchez to St. Louis. It was a well-publicized event. But there was another related incident that hadn't been highly publicized. Another steamboat, the Sultana, had just left the Natchez dock with a packed passenger list. Someone watching the view from the deck had seen the explosion north of them and the Sultana had turned back to help out. According to the account, they had gotten too close and some sparks had spread to the Sultana. The sparks had landed in a set of cotton bales that were in the process of being moved below deck. There were a few passengers on deck, watching the view from the top deck. One woman had been killed. Her name stood out on the page and sent ice water through Bradley's veins.

Erika Becquerel.

His sister had been making a trip to New Orleans. Whatever for? Had she been going to look for him?

The memory of the drunken steamboat captain flashed through his memory eliciting anger along with fear.

He had to stop her. He had to save his sister's life.

Now he had two reasons to return to 1838.

CAMILLE HAD ENLISTED ERIKA'S HELP AND HAD GOTTEN HOME before her father returned from the plantation.

Camille accepted that Bradley had left. She had unpacked his trunk and put the clothes back in the bureau. She did this knowing it was illogical. It was doubtful she would even see him again.

She took the jacket he had worn his last night here and carefully folded it. After running a hand over it, she took it to the bureau and laid it on the shelf where she had put his other jackets. As she turned, an item that didn't fit in caught her attention. She shifted his clothes and found the item. It was the odd britches he'd worn the night he'd shown up wet from the thunderstorm. She pulled out the stiff cloth and shook out the pants. One side was heavier than the other.

Reaching into the left pocket, she pulled out a pocket watch. She recognized it immediately. It was by LeRoy made in Paris. She knew this because her father had a similar one – except her father's was gold and this one was pewter.

She was thankful this one was silver, otherwise she would have suspected that this was, indeed, her father's watch. She stared gave the stem a little twist and stared at the ticking second hand. This was a valuable item and told her a great deal about Bradley. Things he hadn't told her.

First, he came from a family of some means. Second, it told her he had not planned to leave this time. If he had planned to go, he would have taken the watch with him. It was much too valuable to leave behind.

Most importantly, it told her that if it was within his power, he would return to her.

Her face flushed with this new emotion, she retrieved a light shawl from her room, and went out the back door. She walked through the alley down to the river wharf. It wasn't the safest place for a female, but it was broad daylight and if she walked north a little ways, she would come to a little park near some respectable houses. She could be there in twenty minutes.

She lifted her face and enjoyed the feel of the sunlight on

her skin. There was a light breeze coming off the river, putting the odors of the city behind her.

There were several women already sitting on the benches watching their children running and playing. Camille recognized a couple of the women as casual acquaintances. But since she spent most of her time either at the plantation or in the tavern, she wasn't in a position to feel obligated to converse with them.

Instead she found an empty bench overlooking the river and sat, allowing her thoughts to roam.

Like the river, its water choosing its familiar path, with nothing strong enough to veer it off course, her thoughts flowed to Bradley.

She gazed toward the clouds, studying the wispy white streaks and wondered where he was now. What was he doing? Did he ever think of her?

He isn't supposed to be here. Madame Laveau's words drifted back to her.

Bradley had left the room by the time the mystical woman had turned her uncanny gaze on Camille. Camille had steeled herself and bravely kept her seat as Madame Laveau spoke in a deep, eerie voice. Camille had questioned her further.

"What do you mean he shouldn't be here?" she'd asked. "Do you mean in this time?"

She'd waved her hands, encompassing everything. "Here. This time. New Orleans."

"Where then? Where is he supposed to be?"

Madame Laveau had leaned forward and placed a finger beneath Camille's chin. Even the mere memory of the woman's cool, but gentle touch still sent shivers down her spine. "He should be in Natchez near his sister."

Camille pulled her shawl closer, her eyes moist as the memories flooded back.

Madame Laveau had removed her finger then and sat back,

her eyes closed. As the seconds passed, Camille stood up to leave. Perhaps she had nothing more to say.

"And you," Madame Laveau had added.

"Me what?" Camille asked, but the woman had waved her off, dismissing her.

Camille had joined Bradley who had obviously been distraught by the visit with the woman.

Camille's gaze locked onto the horizon. There was something she was missing. "And me what?" she whispered out loud.

Two boys laughed and squealed in the park behind her. Camille felt a painful tug of grief from missing her brothers. Her father stayed busy with the tavern and various business meetings. Her mother preferred the quietness of the planation.

Camille needed to go to the plantation. She needed to talk to her mother.

TWO DAYS LATER CAMILLE SMILED AS SHE FOUND HER MOTHER behind the house dipping candles. Though they had servants for such tasks, Rebecca Lafleur enjoyed doing such everyday tasks herself.

"It keeps my hands busy and my mind quiet," she claimed.

When she saw Camille, her face brightened and she left the candle task to a servant who had been assisting. She put an arm around Camille. "My lovely daughter returns from the city," she said.

"I waited too long," Camille said.

"It's not the same there without your brothers, is it?"

"Nowhere is," Camille realized.

"I feel that way about all three of my children," her mother said. "Come, let's have some strawberry water."

Arm in arm, they strolled to the house and went up the back steps where a servant brought them water and a plate of strawberries. Camille sat back and watched as her mother cut up the fruit and added it to the water. It was odd having others do for her after having become so accustomed to serving others at the tavern.

"I know you didn't come all this way just to sit and drink cold water with me," her mother said.

"And what would be wrong with that?" Camille asked, taking a glass from her mother.

"Nothing. Except that word has it that the young man who was calling on you left to travel to Natchez."

Camille set down her glass. Did her mother know then?

"Some say," Rebecca continued. "that you travelled with him. Others, of course, wouldn't dare spread such rumors."

Camille leaned back in the chair. Her mother knew. But she wouldn't judge her. Rebecca Lafleur understood that things were not always simple.

She suddenly felt safe. Her mother would know what to do. She always did.

"Mother," she said. "You know I've never wanted to get married."

Rebecca smiled. "Who could blame you. Your father only introduced you to the most unattractive of men. Haven't you wondered if maybe he didn't want you to marry?"

Camille's eyes widened. The thought had never even occurred to her. "Surely that's not the case," she said. "Anyway, I think that perhaps that I never wanted to leave my family and marry because I hadn't met the man I wanted to marry."

"And now you have," Rebecca said.

Camille could only aspire to exhibit the calmness her mother did in such situations.

"I'm not sure," Camille said. "Perhaps."

"You have to decide if you're willing to live in Natchez."

"I think you could be a sorcerer," Camille said, a smile

playing about her lips. "You could be right. Except that I don't know if he's still there."

Rebecca frowned. "What do you mean?"

Somewhat relieved that her mother didn't know everything. Camille said, "He's from far away and I don't know where he is."

"Does he have family in Natchez?"

"Yes. His grandmother and his sister."

"Then he'll be back."

Camille looked past her mother turning her gaze to the sky.

That was it. That was the piece she had been missing.

Bradley didn't belong in New Orleans. He hadn't had a reason, really, to be there.

It was only then that she remembered the words Madame Laveau had said as she was leaving. *You beckoned him.*

The words hadn't made sense at the time and Camille had dismissed them, thinking she meant something literal like bringing Bradley to see her.

But, no, she had been telling Camille that Bradley was only in New Orleans to be with her.

And you.

He should be in Natchez with his sister *and me.*

And in that instant, Camille knew she was in the wrong place.

CHAPTER 14

*B*radley checked the clock on his dashboard and shifted in his seat. Driving had lost its appeal years ago – probably the first time he sat in the cockpit of an airplane. He'd been in college at the time. He couldn't remember ever wanting to be anything other than a pilot. Even his Halloween costumes had been pilot uniforms. There was a picture in one his mother's photo albums with him dressed as a fireman. He'd been a toddler at the time, though, so Bradley maintained that he hadn't picked that one out.

And, of course, there had been the kites. Before he'd ever been airborne, he'd been fascinated by kites. He'd become quite good at keeping them in the air. Not that they were anything like keeping an airplane airborne. Nonetheless…

He turned down the long dirt driveway leading to his grandfather's house and his headlights switched on. The drive was shaded by tall oaks creating a leafy tunnel. At the end of the half mile tunnel, the road opened up into a clearing where the house sat. It was nearly dark, but his grandfather was expecting him.

He'd left the porch light on.

Bradley pulled around to the back and parked his SUV. His

grandfather met him at the back door. "It's a long drive," Jonathan said.

"You have no idea," Bradley said, stepping out and stretching his back.

Jonathan chuckled. "I'm not so old that I don't remember how trying a long car trip can be. I will admit, though, you have me spoiled. With you flying me to Monroe to visit your mother, I'm not sure I'd want to tackle the drive again."

Bradley admired his grandfather's tactfulness at not coming right out and asking why he'd driven instead of flying – especially knowing Bradley's aversion to making long trips in the car. He pulled his suitcase from the trunk, took a shoebox from the passenger seat, and draped his new black leather Levenger saddlebag over his head before joining his grandfather.

Bradley lugged his suitcase upstairs and put the shoebox on the desk. He kept the somewhat heavy saddlebag which he wore cross-body style with him. If he'd learned one thing, it had been to be prepared at all times.

Going back downstairs, he stopped in the foyer and stared at the grandfather clock with the scar across its face, the pendulum swinging back and forth.

The clock was hundreds of years old, purchased by his ancestors and shipped over from France.

According to the legend, the clock had been purchased by Nathaniel Becquerel for his wife. There was some sketchiness in the records regarding his wife's name. Nonetheless, the clock had been passed down as a symbol of love starting with Nathaniel.

Jonathan came to stand next to him. "You're here to have another go at it," he said.

"Yep. I guess I am."

His grandfather nodded. "I thought you would. Gave up on New Orleans?"

Bradley shifted and gazed into his grandfather's eyes. "What do you think about that?"

A sadness came over his grandfather's features. "If I could find a way to your grandmother, I would do it. I wouldn't question it. Never would have. I would have done whatever it took to be with her."

"I… She…" Bradley closed his mouth. Did Jonathan know about Vaughn?

He couldn't tell him. Not without having seen Vaughn with his own eyes. He blew out his breath. Even if he had seen her, he wasn't sure he would put his grandfather through that torture. The torture of knowing that someone he loved lived, but in another time.

"If you make it back," Jonathan said. "Tell Vaughn that I still love her and I'm still here. Waiting for her."

Bradley gaped at his grandfather. He did know then.

"But she…"

"No," Jonathan said. "I know she didn't die. I helped her fake her own death. I don't know if she's still alive even… in the past. But if she changed her mind and wants to come home, I'm here."

"You can't go," Bradley said.

"The spell is only for Vaughn and those who carry her blood."

"I'm sorry, Granddad."

"It's ok. She made her choice. She had a reason."

Bradley's heart ached for his grandfather. "If I see her, I'll tell her."

Jonathan nodded and turned away. "I'll be in the kitchen if you need me," he said over his shoulder.

When he got to the door, he stopped, turned around, and came back to draw Bradley into a hug. "Just in case," he said, keeping his eyes downcast. "Know that I love you."

First his mother, now his grandfather. Apparently everyone

expected him to go and never return. Maybe this was a bad idea. He'd struggled with his sister's time-travel. When Erika didn't return, it was as if she had died. He'd grieved. He was certain his grandfather and mother had grieved also. Now Bradley was putting through the same thing.

He went to the back porch, pulled his phone from his bag and pulled up Camille's picture. And his pulse became steadier. This was the right thing.

His grandfather would have done it for Vaughn. Erika did it for Charles.

He would do it for Camille.

He only hoped she would have him.

BRADLEY MOPED AROUND THE HOUSE FOR THREE DAYS. HE KNEW he must look like a madman wearing his saddlebag across his shoulders. Jonathan didn't seem to mind and no one else knew. He didn't even shower for fear that he would suddenly travel through time and not have his things.

He even slept with it on him. At night he charged his phone with an external battery that he kept plugged in during the day.

What sane man would take a cell phone to 1838 anyway?

Nonetheless, he had very good reasons for everything in his bag – even his phone. He had pictures he wanted to show Erika, including a screen image of the article with the steamboat explosion. He wanted to be able to show it to her – anything to keep her from getting on that boat.

And there was the Tiffany's engagement ring he'd selected to give to Camille. She would be a woman ahead of her time.

He walked the halls, stared at Camille's photo, and spent countless hours standing in front of the grandfather clock, inexplicably drawn to its battle scared face.

He officially declared himself insane.

· · ·

"SHOW ME THAT AGAIN," ERIKA SAID.

Camille glanced over and the two women broke into laughter. Knitting, it seemed was not Erika's forte.

It was certainly not from a lack of patience or skill of instruction on Camille's part.

They sat out back, enjoying the fresh air. Charles was out riding in the fields, leaving the women to their own devices.

Erika stopped laughing and turned her head aside.

"What is it?" Camille asked, a feeling of alarm shooting through her.

"Nothing," Erika said. "I must have eaten something that didn't agree with me. I just had a wave of nausea."

"That's two days in a row," Camille said. "Are you sure you're well?"

"Of course," Erika said, but Camille saw the concern in her new friend's furrowed brow.

Mostly in an effort to change the subject, Camille said, "It's going to rain."

Erika laughed. The weather was much too pretty to rain.

"No, I'm serious. See those clouds over there." She pointed behind Erika at the growing black clouds.

"Well, that's not fair," Erika said. "I couldn't see behind me."

"Really?" Camille said. "It seems fair to me." Camille smiled as she used the words Erika had taught her. Since she'd been here for several weeks, she asked Erika to use language from the future and if Camille didn't understand something, she would ask. Erika was surprisingly adept at switching back and forth between the two time periods.

The wind began to pick up, but Camille welcomed the coolness. They knitted in silence for about thirty minutes, with Camille focusing on her own work to avoid laughing at Erika's efforts. In truth, she was worried about her. She hadn't felt well lately and had hardly eaten anything. They had been going for a walk each morning, but for the last few days, Erika had slept in instead.

In the weeks since Bradley disappearance, it seemed like Camille had been on a constant alert – always watching for him. She frequently glanced toward the back door, as though expecting him to appear at any moment. Erika did the same thing when Charles was in the fields.

When Camille thought about Bradley, however, she often inexplicably found herself watching the sky. She supposed it was due to his disappearance. She couldn't think of any other explanation.

The rumble of thunder jarred them out of their contentment and they moved to the back porch. They had no more than sat down again when the rain started.

Camille sat holding her knitting in her lap, looking toward the sky. The rain always brought back an image of Bradley standing in the tavern - a red umbrella in one hand a glass of wine in the other. The image always made her smile.

At Erika's soft gasp, Camille jerked her head back to her friend. Erika was staring at the back door as though she had seen a ghost. Camille followed the direction of her gaze and froze.

She didn't dare blink.

Bradley stood in the open doorway, looking a bit dazed, a leather bag strapped across his shoulders.

Camille had thought about him so much she thought she must be imagining him.

But then she saw his eyes. His beautiful blue eyes.

She jumped up, the knitting needles clattering to the floor along with the yarn, and she ran to him, throwing her arms around him.

"It's you," she said, pulling back, running her hands along his arms.

He smiled back, taking her hands and squeezing as though he would never let go. "Camille," he breathed.

Then Erika was standing next to them. He drew Erika close, hugging them both.

As they stood there, lightening crashed around them and the rain blew under the porch. "I think we should go inside," Erika said.

"I'll be right back," Erika said, then squeezed Bradley's hand. "Don't go anywhere!" she said.

Camille led Bradley into the parlor where they sat together on the sofa. "You're here," she said.

"Finally."

"What took you so long?" She asked.

"I had some things to take care of."

"And did you get those things done?"

"I did," he took her hand, squeezed.

"So you can stay?"

He chuckled. "I hope so. More than anything." He pulled her close and her breath hitched as his lips touched hers.

Once their lips touched, they didn't seem to be able to get enough of each other. Camille wanted to kiss him forever.

But then Erika was back. "Hey, you two. Get a room."

Bradley started to stand up. "Okay," he said.

"I'm kidding," Erika said. "Talk to me first."

Bradley rummaged into his bag. "I brought you something," he said.

Erika grabbed the little black box with an exclamation of delight.

"What is it?" Camille asked.

"It's a cell phone," Erika said as she gazed at it.

"You told me about that," Camille said. "But it won't work, right?"

"Right," Bradley said. "But it also has pictures on it. And…" he said, reaching back into his bag. "I brought something else."

Erika's eyes widened as he handed her a thin black book. "Oh my God! Is it?" She snatched it from him and ran her hand reverently over the back. She opened the cover and gasped, her eyes wide. "You brought an iPad," her eyes teared up as she pressed her fingers against the screen. Camille peeked over her shoulder. It looked like the phone, only larger.

"What does it do?" Camille asked.

Erika wiped at her eyes. "You loaded it with romance novels."

"Of course," Bradley said, smiling broadly.

Erika suddenly looked distressed. "It won't last long. The battery."

"I brought a solar panel charger."

Erika gaped at him. Then her face broke into a wide grin. "My brother the techno genius." She set the iPad down and threw her arms around him. "I love you," she murmured.

"I love you, too," he said and patted his bag. "I brought the money this time," he said, as she moved back to her seat.

Erika glanced up. "You don't need money," she said, tapping on the book.

"Now you tell me," Bradley rolled his eyes.

"Bradley wants to be independent," Camille pointed out.

"I was thinking I could buy a small steamboat and use it to transport things like people and cotton from local plantations and Natchez."

Erika smiled. "You would think of that."

Bradley grinned. "A pilot is always a pilot."

Camille didn't understand this exchange between brother and sister, but she didn't need to. When Bradley met her brothers, he would have a similar experience.

"By the way," Bradley said. "There's an article I downloaded there that you need to read." His voice was serious.

"Sure," Erika said, her eyes still on the iPad.

"Erika," he said. "Look at me." She looked up.

"This is very important. Do not get on the steamboat Sultana."

"Okay," she agreed.

"It's very important."

"I won't. I promise."

LATER THAT EVENING, AFTER THE RAIN HAD PASSED, AND THEY had finished supper, Bradley and Camille sat outside on the porch swing.

"How long are you going to wear that thing?" she asked, indicating his leather bag.

He laughed. "I guess I can take it off now. If anything happens, you'll keep it for me." The money was no good in the future and Erika had commandeered his cell phone. He would have to get a new one if went back to the future.

"Well," Camille said, a smile playing about her lips. "I have something for you."

"Do you now? What is it?" he asked, moving to kiss her.

"Not that." She reached into her skirt pocket and pulled out the silver pocket watch.

"I thought I'd lost it," he said.

"I've been carrying it for you."

"Thank you," he said, kissing her then.

Lost in her kiss, Bradley had no doubt that he was where he was supposed to be.

Here, in 1838, he'd found his place.

And his love. "I love you Camille," he murmured against her lips.

"I love you, too." She sat back, suddenly, gazing into his eyes. "Will you stay?"

"I plan to stay. I don't know how it works. But my heart is here."

"Erika stayed."

"She did and that gives me hope," he said, running his thumb along her lips.

Her eyes closed and she leaned forward.

"Not even time itself will ever pull me away from you again," Bradley promised.

NOW THAT THEY HAD STARTED KISSING, CAMILLE COULDN'T GET enough.

They kissed ALL the time.

Well, not all the time. Erika made sure they had separate bedrooms.

What she didn't know wouldn't hurt her. At least that's what Bradley had said when he'd tapped on her door the second night he'd been back.

She'd opened the door and took a step back. "Someone's going to see you," she whispered as he closed the door behind him and closed the distance between them. He gathered her in his arms. She liked the way her head tucked beneath his chin. And the way he held her close as though he would never let her go.

"Let's go out on the balcony," he said, taking her hand and leading her across the room. "The moon is brilliant tonight."

He opened the French doors and they stepped outside. He was right. The moon was bright tonight. And they sky was lit up with an endless array of stars. "Someday," Bradley said, "we'll be able to fly among the stars and land on the moon."

"You're teasing me again," she said, but in her heart she knew he wasn't teasing. He might be pretending to tease, but that's how he told her things he knew she shouldn't know.

He pulled back and looked in her eyes. "There is something I haven't told you."

"What?" She asked, her heart tripping. He looked so serious. Was he leaving now?

"You probably already know it."

"Tell me anyway," she said. "You can't say that and not tell me."

"Ok," he said, taking both her hands in his. "I'm in love with you."

Her heart soared to the moon. "I'm in love with you, too," she said.

He dug in his pocket and pulled something out. She felt something cool slip onto her finger. He dropped to his knees in front of her and squeezed her hands to his. "Let's get married," he said. "Let's do it now."

"Oh," she said. "Okay." Her blood was pounding so fast in her ears, she could barely think. She'd imagined this moment so many times before, but never like this.

He tugged her to him and she was sitting in his lap. "Do you want to live here?" he asked. "Or in New Orleans?"

"You hate New Orleans."

"I hate New Orleans in the future. Not so much now."

"Not so much," she echoed. Which meant at least a little. "Let's live here for now."

"Good," he said. "I like it here."

"I do, too."

Then they were kissing again.

"Let's get married tomorrow," he murmured against her lips.

Her heart raced. "We can't."

"Why not?" he nuzzled her earlobe sending tingles of fire down her spine.

"I don't know. Why?"

"Because I don't want to wait any longer. I want you to be my wife."

She giggled. "You haven't even asked me yet."

He lifted her hand and the diamond he'd slid on her finger

sparkled in the moonlight. "Camille Lafleur. Will you marry me?"

She gasped, but was too overcome with emotion to speak. "Yes?"

She nodded and felt tears running down her cheeks.

But then he was kissing her again and the tears became a smile. "Don't you have to ask my father first?" she asked, between kisses.

"I'll ask him later."

She giggled. "Ok."

A few minutes later, someone knocked at Camille's door. She clutched at his arms. "What do we do?"

He hesitated, then shrugged. "It doesn't matter. We're getting married tomorrow."

"No," she said, standing up. "I should go."

When Camille opened the door, Villars stood on the other side. "Mistress Erika sent me to bring Bradley to her."

"It's ok," Bradley said, "I'll be right back."

Camille closed her door and went to sit at her dresser. She picked up a brush and began brushing her hair. Running the brush through her hair, she counted to one hundred as her mother had taught her to do. After one hundred brush strokes, she set the brush down and went back outside. She put her hands on the rail and leaned over.

The air was quiet. As she stood there, she heard distant laughter drifting from the staff quarters. Then a dog barked in the distance.

She shivered and went back inside, closing the French doors behind her. She sat on the chair for a few minutes, but her eyes began to grow heavy. She climbed into the bed and hugged the pillow to her. She studied the ring on her finger. Admired the glow of the diamond in the candlelight.

What if Bradley didn't come back?

He'd disappeared once before. That meant it could no doubt happen again.

He wanted to get married. What if she married him and he went back to his time? What then?

Did she call herself a widow? After how long? And what if he made it back years later. How would she explain that?

By the time Bradley knocked lightly on the door, Camille had worked herself into a such a frenzy, she didn't even open the door for him.

He peeked around the corner anyway, then came into the room and went to stand next to her. She didn't resist when he pulled her into his arms.

"What is it ma chère? Why the pout?"

"I thought you weren't coming back."

He held her close, running a hand through her hair. "Yeah. That's actually a valid concern."

She pulled back, looked up at him. "What do we do?"

"We have to have faith that we're meant to be together. And you have to know that if that ever happens, I'll do everything in my power to get back to you. No matter how long it takes."

She shook her head. "I don't know. Maybe we're asking too much."

"You're having second thoughts?"

She closed her eyes tightly. "Just the opposite. I'm wondering how I would live without you."

He smiled at her. "You live. That's how. You live no matter what and I'll find you."

She returned his smile. "Like in the book."

"The book?"

"The Last of the Mohicans."

She saw in his face the moment he remembered the line from the book. "Yes, exactly like the book."

He kissed her on the tip of her nose. "Where do you want to get married, my love?

Camille didn't hesitate. "Beneath the big oak tree with the branches that dip to the ground."

"Perfect," he said.

They stayed up much too late.

Kissing.

Kissing was the nectar of the Gods.

Camille could not be happier.

She was going to be Mrs. Bradley Becquerel.

EPILOGUE

*V*aughn looked around the table and smiled at the laughter of the young people.

She had both her grandchildren with her – Erika and Bradley, as well as their new spouses – Charles and Camille.

Camille had taken to Vaughn immediately, but Charles was still a little wary of her. A lifetime of seeing her as a mystery was difficult to overcome. He was coming around though as the others embraced her.

They had taken to spending more and more time at Vaughn's home during the day. Vaughn had started cooking again, something she had enjoyed in her life with Jonathan and she attributed that as one of the reasons they flocked to her.

Erika was three months pregnant and Vaughn counted the moments until she could hold her great grandchild. Something she never expected to happen.

Vaughn smiled to herself as she reflected on her own two loves – Nathaniel and Jonathan. She missed both of them deeply, but she wouldn't give up anything for any moment she had spent with either of them.

The spell that had sent Vaughn spiraling through time seemed to have settled now that her descendants were here with her. An unexpected twist of fate had brought Erika back in time to be with Charles. Then the stars had aligned to allow Bradley to also come back to her. He had made a stop along the way in New Orleans to pick up Camille, reaffirming Vaughn's belief that love knew no boundaries.

Not even time itself.

Bradley had brought a photo of Jonathan and she kept it on her nightstand. She thought of him often and had grown lonely for him.

Vaughn had begun feeling a little prickly sensation along the back of her neck. One she hadn't felt in quite some time.

She felt it last week and again yesterday.

And just now. Now with her family gathered around her.

Perhaps that had been her purpose in being here in this time. To bring them together.

Now, perhaps, she was free to follow her own destiny.

Want a glimpse at the Becquerel's future? How about a bonus short story?

GET MY BONUS SHORT STORY
https://BookHip.com/QKVHTKD

Turn the page for a preview of
Once in a Blue Moon...

ONCE IN A BLUE MOON PREVIEW
PROLOGUE

*A*s Arabella Becquerel unfolded the letter in her hands, the faded parchment paper crinkled beneath her fingertips. She slid her toes out of her black pumps. Then glancing at the attorney watching her as he finished up a phone call at his desk across the room, slid her foot back into her shoe.

She was confused by the formality of her great-grandmother Vaughn's estate attorney. When her great-grandfather Jonathan died fourteen months ago, the estate had seamlessly passed to her great-grandmother. That was when Arabella learned that Jonathan had put everything he owned in Vaughn's name before they were even married – before his last deployment to Vietnam.

After Jonathan had died peacefully in his sleep at the age of eighty-four, the light had gone out of her great-grandmother's eyes. Arabella was convinced that Vaughn had died of a broken heart. Takotsubo cardiomyopathy.

Arabella's cell phone blinked with a text message. She glanced at her phone resting next to her on the plush dark brown sofa.

How much longer?

Her fiancé, Matthew Caldwell Jennings, III, had been miffed when she'd asked him to wait in the lobby. Even though she was engaged to be married to him and he was an attorney to boot, it hadn't felt right to have him there when the attorney went over Vaughn's estate.

It was something Arabella wanted – needed – to do alone.

Ignoring Matthew's impatience, she opened the letter and blinked back a fresh wave of tears as she recognized her great-grandmother's handwriting.

My dearest Arabella,

Right about now, you're going to be wondering at the mystery surrounding my estate.

Arabella would have smiled under other circumstances. Instead, she swallowed the lump in her throat. Taking a deep breath, she continued reading.

There are things – so many things – I haven't told you. As you read this letter, you'll have a better understanding about why I worked so hard to instill a love of history in you. Why history is so interwoven in our shared blood.

Arabella's eyes blurred with moisture and she put a hand over her eyes. Her throat burned as a sob escaped her fragile self-control. Her tears fell on the paper and smudged the ink of Vaughn's signature at the bottom of letter. Arabella gasped when she noticed her tears on the paper. She wiped at the letter, but only succeeded in smudging the ink and blurring Vaughn's words.

Chapter 1

Turn right in one hundred feet.

Arabella turned onto what looked more like a footpath than a road. "Seriously?" She muttered to herself.

Having grown up in the urban world of Baton Rouge, Louisiana, it was baffling that her great-grandmother had lived here in the countryside outside of Natchez until taking Arabella to raise thirty years ago. It was only more baffling that Arabella didn't know this until after her great-grandmother's death.

She pulled up in front of the house and turned off the motor. The house was a quintessential antebellum mansion. Huge pillars lined the balcony that ran along the whole outside edge of the house. Tall French windows/doors ran from floor to ceiling. The white paint was fresh and spring flowers spilled from pots on the veranda. Unbeknownst to Arabella until three weeks ago, her grandparents had paid a neighbor to keep the house up.

For thirty years.

Her great-grandmother, it seemed, had a surreptitious talent in financial matters.

Her heart ached as she walked up the steps to stand at the front door. She was pretty sure she was the reason her grandparents had moved from here to Baton Rouge, though the reason was lost somewhere within the smudged words of Vaughn's letter to her.

Holding the key in her hand, she hesitated. It was surreal that this house now belonged to her.

She gasped as the door opened, her feet frozen as she fought the urge to run back to the safety of her car. Who could be here in this abandoned house?

A man, maybe mid-sixties, opened the door and grinned at her. "You must be Arabella."

"Yes." She managed to keep her feet planted securely in place. And put what she hoped passed for a smile on her face.

"I'm Jerry."

Ah. The caretaker. "You live here then?"

His eyes widened sheepishly. "Only temporarily. My house flooded out and I needed a place to stay while I basically rebuilt it. My wife is staying with her sister in Jackson. It didn't seem right for us both to be living here."

"It's quite alright," Arabella assured him. "A house breathes better with someone inside."

He sighed with relief. "I didn't get a chance to run it by your great-grandmother on account of her taking sick and all." He lowered his eyes. "I sure am sorry to hear of her passing."

Arabella swallowed the lump in her throat and said the words that were expected. By now they were automatic. "Thank you. It means a lot to me for you to say so."

"Come on in here." Jerry opened the door wide for her to follow him inside.

She stepped into the foyer onto the polished mahogany floor reflecting light from the chandelier above. An odd sense of familiarity swept through her.

She walked to a nearly black rosewood grandfather clock standing next to the staircase and studied its faded dial. The case was decorated with ornate columns. The clock's face wore a jagged rip between the Roman numerals six and seven.

She opened the little glass door and ran her fingertips along the rip.

"I apologize. What?" She realized Jerry was talking, but instead of turning toward him, she kept her gaze on the clock. It was silent. "Is it broken?"

"Oh no. That scar's been there since the Civil War."

"No. The clock. It isn't ticking."

"It's over two hundred years old, but I don't think it's broken. It needs winding, but I don't know where the key is."

Arabella tugged on a platinum chain she wore around her neck and pulled a key from beneath her sweater. She swept the chain over her head, inserted the key, and wound the clock.

"How did you...?" Jerry stopped talking and stood silently as she closed the glass door and the clock began to tick.

"Much better." She said, looking around now. "You were saying?"

"Never mind. If you're going to be staying for awhile, I can make other arrangements."

She turned and met his gaze. "There's no need for that. It's a big house. You'll hardly even know I'm here."

She went up the stairs and stopped on the landing to look out the wavy glass of the eight-foot-high window. The evening sun drifted over the tall pine trees that started a few yards past the lawn. Someone, probably Jerry, kept the lawn manicured. She placed one hand on the thick indigo French brocade draperies tied back on either side. Leaning her forehead against the smooth wooden frame, she rested her eyes.

Her great-grandmother Vaughn had always been prone to flights of fancy. Since Arabella was a child, she had told her tales of the south when the south was in its prime. When men and their ladies attended grand balls, waltzing beneath the moonlight.

What she hadn't told Arabella was that she owned a southern antebellum home. This was no doubt where Jonathan had come when he'd gone on *hunting trips.* Hunting trips that didn't seem to involve any hunting.

Yet her great-grandmother stayed away from here and went to extremes to keep Arabella away.

Jerry followed her up the stairs. "Miss Arabella. There's something else."

Turning, she looked at Jerry who was rubbing the beard on his chin. "What is it?" She smiled. He seemed like a nice man, but he was a nervous sort. "What is it Jerry?"

"Before my house flooded, I'd started renovating the bedrooms. About the time I got everything pulled out, my house flooded, so I haven't gotten back to it. I have some neighbors willing to help if need be, but the renovations are taking longer than I expected. So I'm sleeping in one of the rooms upstairs."

"Okay," Arabella said and continued upstairs.

"So there really isn't any place for you to sleep."

She stopped, looking down the stairs at him. "It's okay. I'll make do." She went upstairs and peeked into each bedroom, one by one. Just as Jerry had warned, the bedrooms were in disarray. All the furniture and art work had been moved into one room. One daybed had been left accessible and the bedding had been left thrown back and a little 12-inch television sat balanced on a chair next to the bed. This was obviously where Jerry was sleeping.

In the remaining rooms, the floors and light fixtures were covered in plastic, the windows and wall outlets were lined with painter's tape, and all the doors had been removed. One room had a set of sawhorses set up and a table saw and other tools as well as planks of wood to replace sections that were damaged.

"These are serious renovations." Without turning, she knew he was behind her, waiting in the hallway.

"I know." His voice held notes of apology. "Miss Vaughn met me in town before she took ill. She wouldn't come near the house, but I showed her pictures of what needed to be done. She knew every inch of this house."

"It's a travesty she didn't come back here."

"Yeah, do you know what happened?"

"I wish I did," Arabella said. "Would you be a dear and find me some bedding? I'll sleep in the parlor."

When he went off to search for bedding, she blew out her breath and walked through the master bedroom. She fervently wished that she could have spent time here with her great-grandparents, Jonathan and Vaughn. The true reason of why they never brought her here and why Vaughn never came near the house may forever be a mystery.

This was her house now and she intended to live here. Eventually.

But... there was much to be done first.

As she turned from the room, she noticed a storm brewing in the distance. The dark clouds were banked among the tips of the tall oak trees.

A flash of lightening was followed seconds later by a rumble of thunder. She shivered.

Chapter 2

Colonel Augustus Townsend stood on the veranda of the plantation house and watched as his men turned what had been immaculate grounds into a Confederate camp replete with tents, fires, and horses everywhere.

They'd ridden hard for three days. The horses needed to rest. The Union forces were tightening their ranks around Vicksburg. Augustus needed to get his men there before the fighting started, but they were still a full four day's march out.

Augustus was Southern through and through. He'd grown up in the South and with the exception of three years at West Point, he'd lived his entire life in the south. His job as a soldier was to protect the people of the south – his people. As far as he was concerned, that was the whole point of this damnable war.

Behind the house looked like a refugee camp. As they passed through small towns and farms on their northern trek from New Orleans to Vicksburg, he saw it as his duty to warn the people that the war was coming to their doorstep.

Most of the war was to their east - Atlanta, West Virginia - he'd give them that, but the war was here, too. Without soldiers to protect them, the people would be exposed. He encouraged them to follow his troops to Vicksburg. Once they were safely there, he and General Pemberton's men together, could defeat the enemy. On the ground of their choosing.

In the hour since their arrival, Augustus had determined that this house belonged to Charles and Erika Becquerel. Charles was fighting – somewhere - and his wife had gone to stay for the duration of the war in New Orleans with her sister-in-law.

Nonetheless, the house was teaming with people. The Becquerels appeared to be his kindred spirits. They turned no one away from their door, including the servants that they had set free.

He'd told the older black man, Villars, that they should pack their necessary things and go to Vicksburg. He'd said they would consider it. Thirty minutes later, the house was rife with people carrying who-knew-what here and there.

One thing he'd learned in his travels as a soldier – there was no accounting for what people deemed *necessary items.*

Chapter 3

"The Yankees are coming!"

Arabella stirred on the couch in the parlor. She was dreaming a most peculiar dream.

"Mistress, get up, the Yankees are coming."

Arabella opened her eyes and stared into the deep brown eyes of a dark skinned young woman wearing a long dress and scarf wrapped around her head.

With a quick glance around the room, she realized she was in the parlor of the house bequeathed to her by her great-grandparents.

Her host, Jerry, hadn't said he was having visitors, but then Arabella hadn't asked.

The look in the woman's wide eyes, though, was nearly hysterical.

"What Yankees?" Arabella sat up, pulling the blanket securely around her shoulders.

"Mistress, I ain't knowing who you are, but it don't make no never mind. We's packing up now and we be leaving at first light."

Perhaps the woman had some type of psychosis. Arabella saw this kind of thing from time to time in her work at the hospital. Unfortunately, Arabella didn't have any Haldol with her.

Someone scurried past, behind them. It was then that Arabella noticed that the woman standing over her wasn't the only person showing signs of hysteria. Men, women, and children, black and white, were rushing to and fro carrying items of dubious content around the house.

"It looks disorganized." She muttered to herself.

"Don't say I didn't warn ya." The woman turned and hurried off toward the foyer.

Arabella sat in awe as she watched the people rushing about. All she could think was that they were in serious need of triage training. She wondered if anyone knew what anyone else was doing.

She needed to find Jerry to see what was going on. Perhaps this was part of the renovation process. If so, it certainly explained why it was taking so long. *Longer than expected,* he'd said.

She reached into her pocket and pulled out her cell phone. She'd forgotten to call Matthew, her fiancé, last night to let him know that she'd arrived safely.

It was just as well. Her phone was barely charged and the words *No Service* made it clear that she wouldn't be calling anyone.

Keep reading Once in a Blue Moon...

Kathryn Kaleigh is the author of sixty-eight novels, over one hundred short stories, and many collections.

kathrynkaleigh.com